The Engines of Eros

Timothy Black

Winnipeg, Canada

Developmental editor: Craig Gibb
Proofreader: Francisco Feliciano

Published August 2024 by Deep Desires Press.

Deep Desires Press
PO Box 51053 Tyndall Park
Winnipeg, Manitoba R2X 3B0
Canada

Visit http://www.deepdesirespress.com for more scorching hot erotica and erotic romance.

The Engines of Eros

Before

Rebellious Liberty Ship captain Charlotte Frost and her sentient Doll, Arslan Tash, fled the Matriarchy's grasp only to discover a hidden temple of Ishtar buried under the Syrian Desert. Within an ancient cavern they found a sprawling complex of techno-magic dating back thousands of years. The Matriarchy had stolen its secrets and freed the sole prisoner the Temple was built to contain. But amid these revelations the Temple alerted them to trespassers. Fearing the Matriarchy had tracked them down, the group rushed to confront the threat.

Now

Chapter 1

The walls glowed blue as the mechanical woman and the human aviatrix ran through the Temple of Ishtar. Hundreds of feet below the Syrian Desert the stifling heat was absent, even without the temperature control of the artificial corridors and rooms. Alien script danced below the blue glaze that covered the walls, the reflection patterns forming text readable by anyone who knew the Kurian language. Occasionally, the walls would pulse red, leaving behind ripples of purple as the Temple called out for help.

Intruders had breached the Temple.

Charlotte Frost, captain of the Liberty Ship *Harlot's Promise* and outlaw of the Matriarchy, began to regret still wearing her dark scarlet flight leathers as they rounded a corner in the hallway. On the windswept decks of an airship the flight suit provided warmth as well as protection from the occasional accident, but in a foot race they became hot and uncomfortable all too rapidly. Charlotte was shorter than Tash by nearly a foot, with raven-lock tresses and brown eyes flecked with green. She never knew who her father was, but her tawny-gold skin had contrasted starkly with her mother's pale countenance to such an extent that some believed mother and daughter unrelated. But a quick check of the same oval features of both dispelled that notion quickly.

Next to the aviatrix was her faithful companion, a mechanical wonder of gold and ivory animated with tantric magic. But this Doll was even more unlike her steel and brass counterparts, in that she possessed intelligence and emotions. As if to double down on the oddity, Tash had not one, but two souls, one of them the curvaceous Amazon that ran next to her beloved captain. The other, Arslan, slumbered below the surface, an ancient being who had lost most of his memories when Tash was forced into the same clockwork body. Although he was not as loyal as his female counterpart to Captain Frost, he had made his peace with her to the ends of mutual survival.

"Tash, I hope you know where you're going!" Charlotte huffed, trying to match the boundless stamina of her friend. "The *Harlot's Promise* is still caught in the cavern hangar, and Shamhat is too busy communing with her broken column to be of any use!"

Unlike her mistress, Tash had no breath to lose, the illusion of such as artificial as her musculature. "In my first interface with the Temple I made it a point to download the map of this place. There is one egress point to the surface, a series of stairwells only partially collapsed."

"Only...partially," Charlotte panted. "You...spoil me."

Tash laughed, carefree. "If you wish, mistress, we could awake one of the Enkidu to clear the way."

Charlotte shuddered, a chill passing over her even as

she sweated. "One of those monsters? If you ever want another kiss, then don't...summon those things."

Enkidu were worker frames, piloted by worker sprites the Kurians had created. The scorpion-like mechanicals were the size of a small horse, with a tail holding a variety of tools. The Temple had been stocked with them in case the prisoner got loose, but the Matriarchy helped the entity escape under their noses.

The stairwell was as strange as the rest of the facility, smooth and sloping upward. Despite the angle, the floor wasn't slick, and Charlotte found the angle easy to climb. Tash almost seemed to glide upward along the floor, as if she was ice skating. Each step took her several feet farther than it should have. It surprised and delighted her, and Tash couldn't help but to return and spin around the struggling Charlotte.

"Show-off," Charlotte laughed, stopping to catch her breath. The alarm chimed again. "Can you shut that off?"

Tash nodded. "Of course, mistress. My apologies."

Concentrating for a moment, the clockwork courtesan held her hand out. Dozens of tiny golden needles extended from her palm, waving in as if grain in a breezy field. She then placed her hand against the glowing blue wall. A slight pulse of teal radiated out from there and the alarms quieted a moment later.

"If only it was so easy to deal with the intruders above," Charlotte lamented. "Do you have any information available on them?"

Tash shook her head. "I am sorry, but no. The ruins above are not connected to the Temple system currently.

For the most part, it appears they never truly were. The Kurians built this place to siphon off the sexual energy of unsuspecting worshippers, so they kept most of their magical technology out of sight and construction."

"You make it sound so sinister," Charlotte said, wondering again exactly what the Kurians were and what they wanted with the energy. "Not saying you're wrong, I just wish I knew where your people came from and what their ultimate goal was."

Tash shook her head again. "Not *my* people, mistress. Perhaps they are Arslan's, as he claims, but I feel no filial loyalty to the concept. I am yours, mistress. Not theirs."

The aviatrix blushed, taken aback by the simple yet powerful words. She was still mourning the separation from her cheating wife, Lauren, and the six months since then had been lonely. To have someone declare themselves so quickly and completely after a drought of emotion was sometimes difficult to comprehend, even for a tantric engineer.

"You keep that up, and you're going to blow up my ego and make me feel a bit too special," Charlotte said with a feigned grousing tone. She was surprised when Tash tenderly took Charlotte's face in her hands.

"I could never make you feel as special as you are to me, mistress," Tash cooed, gently brushing her golden lips over Charlotte's. Despite being made of gold and alabaster the magic animating her made the Doll feel as real as a flesh and blood being, and her ghost of a kiss sent Charlotte's nerves tingling all the way down to her toes.

"Keep that up, and we'll never make it to the top of this

stairwell," Charlotte breathed into her companion's lips. Despite the sheer need she felt physically, the logical part of the aviatrix was terrified of what was coming from above. She felt as if she existed on the edge of a sword. On one side lay carnal pleasures with Tash, ignoring the world until it burned down. On the other, the fear of exactly what unknown force was coming.

To the surface world, the ruins of the Temple above were centuries-old and of no interest. At the most, locals would likely think them haunted and avoid the area. After all, no Muslim of good faith would ever tread foot on the sinful lands of the old gods, likely having stories of evil witches and the like inhabiting the ruins. From certain points of view those old legends weren't far off, as the only way religious folk could comprehend the massive complex hidden under the sands was through myth and monsters.

Who, then, would violate whatever local customs and fears protected this place to disrupt the ruins enough to set off alarms in the expansive hidden base underneath? The system would not be so sensitive as to pick up animals and natural settling of debris, as that would make it nearly useless for detecting real threats. Who, then, or what, could be tearing through the upper levels with such single-mindedness as to set off a system-wide alarm?

The thoughts of the danger approaching helped Charlotte break off her embrace with Tash, who gave a little mewl of disappointment that sent a fluttery feeling to the aviatrix's stomach. Even the smallest of habits and emotions from the Doll felt powerfully seductive. If Charlotte made the mistake of kissing her for too long or tasting any of the ambrosia nectar that lay between the Doll's legs, she would truly be lost to the world. Tash possessed a sexual venom that she had little control over that was capable of enslaving even an aviatrix to her will.

They started up the spiraling incline once more. Charlotte's legs were burning with the effort, her stomach was rumbling, and her throat was dry. She hadn't stopped for a meal since they'd fled the flying city Godmother. Although the rush of constantly using her tantric magic had masked physical considerations, there was only so long she could go without tending to the needs of her body. Even Tash had been offline for a few hours while Charlotte had disabled the suppression field that made the Temple uninhabitable. The sudden effort of a run up a winding ramp was quickly draining what little energy the aviatrix had left.

"Go…go on without…me," she gasped, collapsing to her knees. She felt like she needed to throw up, but nothing came but hacking coughs.

"Mistress!" Tash cried in sympathy, going to her knees next to Charlotte, cradling her lady in her lap. "I am so sorry, I forgot the limitations nature has placed on you."

The aviatrix gave a raspy laugh. "Yeah, we flesh and bloods are funny that way. I kind of lost track of my own needs in the excitement of discovery. But forget all that. You've got to stop whatever threatens the Temple. After that's sorted, we can worry about finding our way back to the hangar and the ship."

Tash shook her head. "No, I will not let you lay here starving and in pain while I—"

"Enough!" Charlottes managed to interrupt. "There are more important things here than my comfort. Go, find out what's irritating the Temple…then if you really want, bring me a sandwich."

Both giggled. Tash nodded her assent, kissing Charlotte's hands before releasing them. She then rose and glided up the incline, out of sight. Charlotte could hear the whoosh as the automaton moved more quickly than the captain could ever match, skating as if on ice up the corridor. The sounds faded from earshot as the Doll ascended the spiral.

Charlotte felt woozy and hitched herself over to the softly-glowing wall. It didn't respond to her touch as it had to Tash's, the carved figures underneath flickering at the ready for the Doll's caress. But it was nicely warm against her back, and the floor itself was slightly springy to the touch.

Back the way they'd come were two Enkidu, one to each side, released from their glass storage to serve as eternal sentinels. They were impressive, but utterly useless. Out of three power cores for the Temple, one was missing most of its data diamonds, one was destroyed, and the other struggled to keep the lights on. Charlotte mused how she had blown the mystical embers alive and how it had spread to the other gems to activate them. A small amount of her magic traded for a much bigger reaction.

"So much for the Second Law of Thermodynamics," Charlotte laughed. "Then again, if magic didn't break the rules, it wouldn't be so much fun."

She gave another laugh that a drunkard would have

been proud of. The aviatrix was struggling to stay awake, but the short sprint from the power chamber to here had taken the last of her reserves. She was running on no sleep, no food, and no water for the past thirty hours or so. Multiple orgasms had refueled her mystic abilities, but they had also taken a toll on her physical form. Sleeping after good sex wasn't only convenient, it was necessary.

Despite her best efforts, the aviatrix dozed off. The steady pulse of magic in the Temple, the soft lighting, and the boredom of waiting combined to lull her into sleep against her will.

Nightmares of loss and falling greeted her. Dreams of finding Lauren cheating on her, even after they'd both agreed to stop seeing the hateful Major Enright, dogged her like hounds on the chase. But a gentle pulse of love threaded the bad dreams, and somehow Charlotte was able to hold onto those threads. Soon the dreams turned to a pleasant oblivion, the nightmares becoming less effective than shadows on a wall. The smell of meat and potatoes cooking seeped into her dream, the taste of a hearty stew waking her.

She was nestled in Tash's arms while the automaton held a cooling spoon of stew at her lips, feeding the aviatrix as one would a small child. Sleep kept trying to creep back into Charlotte's eyes. Her muscles were sore with protest, and it felt as if her skin was an iron suit encasing her.

"What…" Charlotte started to say but couldn't get more out than that. Her eyelids were fighting to close, to send her back to the land of sleep.

The stew was delicious, and the spice blend reminded Charlotte of the time she spent in England rescuing people with the *Harlot's Promise*. Happier times, when she'd still been with Lauren, when she'd still believed in the Matriarchy and what it represented. Their Liberty Ship flying through the skies, fast and free, transporting the outcast, the rebellious, the free thinkers from the clutches of those who would do them harm to safe enclaves of like-minded folk.

A small campfire crackled nearby, and a worn tin coffeepot bubbled where it had been hung to brew. As Charlotte's eyes adjusted, she realized they were on the surface, and it was nighttime. A canopy of stars, far too many to count, were splashed across the moonless night. There was a bite in the chilly desert air, and the scrub brush that had been gathered for the fire burned fragrant with a pungent odor.

Charlotte was bundled up in a patched blanket, swaddled and held by Tash. The spoon and bowl were simple tin like the coffeepot, bent and scratched by years of use. In a rush of memory, Charlotte thought of the intruders.

"Tash, what's—"

"Oh, mistress, you are awake," Tash said loudly, drawing raised eyebrows from the aviatrix. "Our *friends* will be so overjoyed."

Taking the hint, Charlotte looked more closely at their surroundings. Two hiking packs were open nearby, the things filled near to bursting with a variety of tools and supplies. A scrawny log had been rolled near the fire to provide ready-made seats.

And there were two men staring at them from it.

The first was a rough sort, scarred, with his unshaven face bristled with gray hair and a pair of uneven mutton chops. Here and there was a touch of what must have once been a fiery red in both his whiskers and his thinning hair. His dirty trousers were patched in multiple places, and the boots he wore were long past their prime. The man scratched himself as he watched them, his stained shirt open to the fingernails that had never seen proper care. Stained teeth broke into a smile that was less than reassuring. The rough man's companion, however, could not have been more different.

The other man was dressed in the fashion of a Londoner, wearing an olive drab tweed suit with a Windsor knot tie and soft cap. But that was where the coifed appearance ended, for the boots he wore were tough and well-used, bearing scratches from an adventurous life. The man himself was dark-skinned, much more so than Charlotte, and where his companion rarely saw a razor, he was clean-shaven and well-tended. He had broad features and a full mouth, which even now was curved into a shy smile, as if he were afraid of showing too much of himself to the world. His eyes were a dark brown, and even behind his horn-rimmed glasses they glittered in the firelight with intelligence and humor. He carried a straight black cane with a brass handle on the top with a pair of soft black leather gloves.

"Lookee there, the fancy 'un woke the little 'un with her feeding," the bigger man said, giving a guttural laugh at his own joke. There was a nasty undercurrent of leering violence, but what surprised Charlotte was the twang of a

Southern man from the Americas. Ever since the Bright had spread across the Atlantic Ocean over twenty years before there'd been no contact with the western hemisphere.

"How did—" Charlotte started to say, before Tash cut her off again.

"You hit your head on rubble, mistress, as we were exploring the ruins, remember?" Tash said with a subtle hint of warning. "These fine gentlemen found me rooting in the stones and offered their campfire to mend you."

"I been many things, little missy, but a gentleman ain't never been any of them," laughed the big man. "Jackson Knox, ma'am." He made no move to get up, merely nodded his head as he poked the fire and spit to the side.

"And, uh, I'm Gabriel Harper," the smaller Black man said, pushing himself off the log and offering his hand eagerly. Charlotte managed to free a hand from the blanket and shook the proffered one. His grip was strong and certain, and the aviatrix immediately liked him.

"They have come over from…Tennessee, was it?" Tash said.

"Georgia, actually," Gabriel corrected her. Unlike Jackson, his speech was clipped and terse, every vowel and consonant pronounced painfully correct. But now that Charlotte knew to look for it, she could detect the twang hiding under his words as well.

"Captain Charlotte Frost," the aviatrix said with a nod, then caught herself, but a moment too late.

"'Captain' you say?" Jackson snickered. "How's that work? Y'all giving out commissions to skirts in these parts?

Then again, I s'pose that ain't any stranger than your nuts-and-bolts servant there."

"That is quite enough of that," Gabriel said tersely, tapping his cane on the ground.

Jackson ducked his head low as if to ward off a blow.

"Didn't mean nothing by it, boss," he said meekly. The dirty white man got to his feet at another tap of the Black man's cane on the ground. "I'll just go on and double check the charges, then. M'apologies, ma'am."

Jackson stumbled away from the camp in the half-light, as if afraid of something. Charlotte sat up and rubbed her eyes to make sure she hadn't imagined the exchange.

"I am an exacting employer," Gabriel said with a tilt of his head. "First time seeing a Black man order a white redneck around without fists flying?"

Charlotte looked at Tash, who shrugged. The Doll had no frame of reference, but the aviatrix remembered her history lessons about the Deep South and the proliferation of slavery there. For a country that prided itself on liberty for all, the horrid practice was a blemish that had tainted it since its founding.

"Money," Gabriel explained. "It is the most magical thing in the world for smoothing over your path. Although, perhaps, not half as wonderous as your clockwork friend."

Tash bobbed her head in a small curtsy at the compliment.

"I assume there is a story to both her and your title, Captain?" Gabriel said, with no trace of the humiliating humor that had infested Jackson's tone. It was impossible that he hadn't encountered similar problems as a well-heeled gentleman of color in Georgia. That he was making a point of extending courtesy to Charlotte was not lost to her.

"Indeed," Charlotte said, sitting upright and shrugging off the blanket. The ruby control gem on her forehead glittered in the firelight. That and the scarlet flight leathers would have clearly marked her for any European, but there was no telling how much of the aviatrixes and the Matriarchy a foreigner from American shores knew of.

"We both have stories to tell, I'd wager," she continued. "We haven't heard anything from the other side of the Atlantic for decades. How, then, did you come to these lands? And, of all places, here?"

"Based on your companion's appearance and your own, I suspect we have both come in search of the same thing."

At Charlotte's blank look, he reached behind him in the pack and pulled out a book packed with extra loose paper stuffed between its dog-eared pages. Unlocking the clasp with a small key he pulled out he opened it, flipping through it until he smiled. He handed the book over, tapping the illustration with a gloved finger.

"We're here to find that: what ancient scholars referred to as an Engine of Eros."

Charlotte let out a breath in surprise. The book Gabriel had presented her bore crude illustrations of a familiar sight.

The Engine of Eros was the diamond-studded pillar that powered the Temple of Ishtar.

Chapter 2

Or rather, it was one of the three. There was no way of knowing if the referenced Engine was the blackened one that had been destroyed, the intact one, or the pillar whose data diamonds the Matriarchy had stolen that contained the prisoner who had taken the name Godmother and directed the flying city-home of the aviatrixes.

"You have seen this, yes?" Gabriel asked excitedly, taking note of her reaction.

Charlotte tried to cover her recognition of the sketch, but it was already too late. Gabriel's eyes were sparkling with excitement, and there was an odd weight to the air as he repeated his question again. During the pause he threw a tightly bound sheaf of grass into the fire, eliciting a brief flash of fire and smoke. The smell of the campfire was giving Charlotte a headache; the plants they'd used had produced an oily smoke that made her eyes sting. Gabriel poured the coffee into a battered cup before offering it to Charlotte.

"Of course, I've seen it; I just didn't know what it was called," Charlotte said before clapping her hands over her mouth with a shocked expression. She hadn't meant to say that. But before she could stop them the words had flown of their own volition from her.

"Excellent," Gabriel breathed. He sat on the end of the log where Tash held Charlotte, and likely would have scooted closer if not for the warning look from the automaton. Instead, he leaned close enough to give the cup of coffee to Charlotte.

Gabriel's cologne was dusky and rich, so overwhelming that Charlotte couldn't even smell the acrid campfire anymore. She downed the coffee as fast as she could, doing her level best to keep her mouth from blabbing more secrets.

"Mistress, are you well?" Tash asked, concern marring her perfect features. In a lower voice she whispered, "I thought we were going to be discreet in discussing the local ruins?"

"I don't know what's going on," Charlotte whispered back, her face flushed.

"What are we talking about?" Gabriel whispered as he leaned in, far too close.

Tash gently moved Charlotte so that her back was supported by the bench-log. Then she suddenly sprang into action, moving faster than a striking serpent, ivory hand grabbing Gabriel by the throat as she stood up. With no apparent effort, the Amazonian machine picked the smaller man up by his throat, her face creased with anger and worry.

"What game are you playing at?" Tash demanded, shaking the man like a dog with a chew toy. "Her response time is down, she is visibly confused about what she is saying, and the words have started to slur together. My mistress is none of these things normally. So, I will ask one single time before I rip your throat out: what are you doing to her?"

For his part, Gabriel was gasping for air, unable to answer, his feet flailing uselessly. He reached into his coat pocket and pulled out a brown glass bottle. As his face began to turn an unhealthy color, he managed to smash the bottle against Tash's arm.

A bubbling blue liquid splashed across the Doll like a paint streak on her alabaster skin. Sparks danced across the surface of the liquid, and suddenly Tash dropped Gabriel. He collapsed wheezing, clutching his bruised throat. Tash's right arm hung limp at her side while she stared at it, visibly perplexed as to why it wasn't responding.

Charlotte coughed, her head spinning, and the cup of coffee tumbled from her hands. She managed to struggle upright and threw the blanket off, pulling the heavy wrench off her tool belt. The aviatrix stumbled over to stand over Gabriel, threatening him with the tool.

"What...what did you just splash on her?" she asked, hefting the wrench to enunciate her point. The world swam in a sickening way, but she concentrated on the crumpled man, making him the focus of all her efforts. Paranoia said she should be on the lookout for his larger, more imposing companion, but there was a limit to what she could manage for some reason.

"Liquid...liquid lightning," Gabriel managed to gasp out, grabbing his cane as if to fend off the wrench she was threatening him with. "Works...to shut down any mechanical threat..."

Tash poked her dead arm, brow furrowed in worry.

"Will it wear off?" Charlotte asked with heavy menace.

Gabriel scooted back to where the other log lay.

"Probably," he shrugged, his voice hoarse. He held the cane out like a fencing sword, and Charlotte could see it was hollow. She didn't want to find out exactly what he had secreted within, but for Tash she was willing to risk it. "I have never seen anything like your friend before. But she was strangling me."

When Charlotte looked back at Tash, Gabriel surreptitiously reached back to get another bundle of grass for the fire. The aviatrix noticed his movement out of the corner of her eye and struck before he could raise the cane, bringing the wrench down on his left forearm with a sound like a branch breaking as he tried to throw the fuel into the fire.

Gabriel gave a short grunt of pain, dropping the grass and twisting away from her to get out of striking range, his cane rolling away as he instinctively cradled his broken arm.

On a hunch, Charlotte reached into the rear of her tool belt, pulling out a portable rebreather she normally used when dealing with engine fires. As soon as she pulled it over her mouth her head began to clear. She bent over and picked up the bundle of grass that Gabriel had been about to throw into the fire.

Even through the mask she could smell some of the sickly-sweet aroma, and she didn't need her perceptor to see that this wasn't just shrub grass he was burning. It was tightly wound, with a greasy feel to the stalks that numbed her fingers slightly.

"What is this?" she demanded, holding the grass bundle out to the man.

Gabriel brought himself up straight where he was sitting, cradling his left arm with a wince. He was looking over at his cane, clearly wondering if he could make the distance before Charlotte. "What do you mean?"

Tash walked over, her dead arm still dangling listlessly.

"If you are counting on your friend to save you, I saw him go into hiding when my mistress broke your arm," Tash said grimly. "Please do bear in mind I still have a functioning arm with which to snap your neck, with plenty of reasons to follow through on that action. Answer Captain Frost. For your health."

"I've been threatened by far worse than you," Gabriel laughed in a mocking tone. Apparently giving up on reaching the cane, he instead pulled himself upright to sit on the log. "Still, as resistant as I am to such things, I feel the compulsion to tell the truth. That's what the grass bundles do. A simple alchemical treatment to certain weeds in this land produces a combination that when burned forces the truth from those inhaling it."

Charlotte and Tash shared a guarded look.

"What exactly were you planning?" Charlotte asked in a carefully neutral tone, finger tapping on the wrench.

Gabriel gave a genuine laugh through his pain. "Oh, nothing like that, I assure you. I simply meant to interrogate you about the Temple of Ishtar. And do not insult my intelligence by feigning ignorance of this location."

"How do you mean?" Charlotte asked, trying to ascertain exactly how much the man knew.

"I said not to do that. Please. There is nothing else for miles around, other than that sad little town on the river," Gabriel said, wincing as he straightened his arm. "Hand me the snuffbox at the top of my pack, would you?"

"So that you can pull an explosive or worse from it?" Tash said, suspicion lacing her words. She toed the cane further away from the man.

"Oh, that would make me a genius, would it not?" he replied with a sneer. "Unless I wanted to kill myself as well, any detonation this close would do us all in. No, it is merely some healing herbs. As proof of my harmless intentions, there's also a small felt sack, red in color, in there. It has a chalky powder that will neutralize the liquid lightning I inflicted on you."

Charlotte nodded for Tash to investigate the backpack that had been laid nearby while she watched Gabriel. He merely sat there, cradling his arm, smiling at her. The scent from the campfire was still heady, and mask or not Charlotte didn't trust herself to talk until the treated grass fully burned away. Tash quickly found the powder that would negate the odd sparking liquid on her arm. As soon as she rubbed the powder in the liquid lightning froze in place mid-spark. A moment later it appeared to dry, and it began flaking off in dirty blue clods. Tash moved her arm experimentally, apparently having regained full function. She nodded at the peace offering and went back to rummaging in Gabriel's pack.

"Is this it?" Tash asked, presenting a small, lacquered box.

"That is indeed the ticket."

Tash looked at Charlotte, who grudgingly nodded. Gabriel slid open the top, revealing some dry yellow and green flakes. He placed the box on his lap and began to unbutton the shirt sleeve cuff on his broken left arm.

"Do you require assistance?" Tash asked, her expression softening somewhat.

"No," Gabriel grunted. "Although it hurts, I doubt either of you have experience with this sort of thing."

Charlotte rolled her eyes. "No, of course such prim and proper ladies as tantric engineers have never had to set a broken bone or seen the sight of blood. Eek. Tash, can you locate his smelly friend and make sure he's not up to some sort of mischief out there?"

The Doll nodded, turning to seek the night with eyes that needed no light to see.

Watching her go, Gabriel had an impish look. He whispered to Charlotte, "Who said anything about a bone?"

As she watched the man began rolling up his sleeve from the gloved wrist. It took a moment for what he was revealing to sink in.

"Is that…" Charlotte started. "Wait, are you…is your arm made of *wood*?"

The span of arm Gabriel had revealed was not skin of any shade. It was smooth and polished, but the wood grain was obvious. Where Charlotte had struck with her wrench there were cracks spiderwebbed out around an impact point. There was a fluid leaking out from the cracks, which at first Charlotte took to be sap of some type. But the firelight flared, and she saw in an instant that the wooden arm wasn't dripping sap.

It was blood.

The mystery deepened when she saw Gabriel flex his gloved fingers in pain as he treated his damaged arm.

"What are you?" Charlotte asked, aware of how blunt a question that was.

"I am...complicated," Gabriel chuckled. He crushed the yellow and green flower petals into his wound, and within seconds it had healed up and stopped bleeding. Flexing his arm experimentally, he stood and sighed in relief.

"Your arm is made of *wood*," Charlotte pressed. "Plant, tree, barking all the way, wood. It doesn't make sense. I saw you flex that hand, use it beyond any ability of a prosthetic. Your fingers *moved*."

Gabriel gave a grim grin. "It's not the only part of me that is composed of plant matter. Do you know what a good ol' plantation owner in Georgia does with a slave who refuses to bow down? Nothing good, I assure you. But my grandfather was a powerful practitioner in the ancient ways, and I was his chosen successor. And one day, the old spells and traditions just started working. No fanfare, no light in the sky. Just one day they were harmless superstitions, and then the next I was able to graft replacements for what the ol' massa took from me."

He rolled down his sleeve, fastening the buttons at his wrist, and made sure none of his wooden limb showed.

"And then," Gabriel mused, holding up his clenched fist, "I took things from him."

Rather than dwell on what exactly he meant, Charlotte changed the subject.

"The Bright. You came through it? I thought it was impassable to all," she said. "They say it glitters like a sunset on the waves, but across the entire sky. A border of fractured light that stretches across the entire Atlantic. Ships that enter never come back."

Gabriel picked up a stick and poked the dying embers of the campfire, making it whoosh as he turned over a half-burnt branch. "Have you ever seen it?"

It was Charlotte's turn to laugh. "I'm not that stupid. Even the matriarchy keeps its distance."

"What if you didn't have a choice?"

Charlotte shook her head. "There's always a choice. I'm guessing from your insinuations you were an escaped slave. Why not just head North?"

"You think that's a safe place?" Gabriel asked. There was no laughter to the question, just a deep tiredness. "The common man only loves us at a distance. An Abolitionist is put to the test when we try for the same jobs, when we live where they live, and when we…love those that we aren't supposed to love."

"But surely there's better options than the Bright," Charlotte argued.

"How much of the Atlantic on this side do you think it covers?" Gabriel asked. "I'll answer as a man who's seen it. Europe can still ply the sea with trade. They have a wide berth. But in the Americas there are places where the shimmering edge of it can almost be seen by land. It's easy to accidentally sail into the Bright without warning. And once in…"

"What?" Charlotte asked, her attention well and fully caught. "What's it like in there?"

Gabriel laughed. There was a manic edge to it. "I cannot even begin to describe what I saw. What we sailed through. There are no words that can capture it, no words that can describe the terrible knowledge you gain as a result. Most of my crew did not make it. Several threw themselves overboard to their end rather than face that maelstrom. Looking into that abyss…you are never the same afterward. Never."

He poked the fire listlessly, caught in whatever memories the Bright had given. The treated grass had burned away, and the aviatrix felt the air had cleared enough to take her rebreather off, folding it up and putting it back in her belt.

Charlotte didn't know what to say to break the silence. She was loathe to have Gabriel return to the badgering questions about the Temple and its secrets. But the change from the self-confident inquisitive man to the morose one poking at the fire was both unexpected and uncomfortable. She reasoned there was no harm in indulging some of his curiosity, if nothing else to make a better companion at the fireside. He was quite attractive, and it had been a long time since she had even been around a man, let alone one that had sailed the Bright. Gabriel's smile was easy, and there was a part of Charlotte that desperately wanted it to light the man's face again. There was a pang of guilt as she recognized the attraction. Thoughts of Tash clouded into her mind, and she couldn't help but think of how her own wife had betrayed her. Charlotte wasn't sure exactly what she and Tash were, but she refused to bring the same pain to the sultry automaton. Even a tantric aviatrix couldn't quite explain the mechanics of attraction and why certain people worked with others, but she could choose to bury that attraction rather than enflaming it. Still, there was little point to sharing a campfire with a sullen man when she could distract him.

"You asked about my title of Captain?" Charlotte said, interrupting Gabriel's musings. She was careful to show a little more cleavage, just enough to entertain without promising anything more.

"Oh, yes," he said, brightening a little. His eyes flicked briefly down, but Charlotte watched him force them back up. "My own was purchased with blood, a stolen Confederate ship, and old-world magic."

"Well, mine was certainly different than that," Charlotte said, watching the embers dance. "My title was granted by lies and betrayals of a more social version. My wife—"

"Wife?" Gabriel interjected, his eyebrows raised in surprise. The same brief flash of lust that nearly every man had rippled across his face. But, like his eyes, Gabriel quickly took hold of the emotion and shut it away. The aviatrix was impressed by just how fast the man was able to rein in the thoughts he did not want. That sort of self-control was rare in the males she'd encountered.

"Yes, wife," Charlotte smiled. Although the temptation was there to tease him a little, she reasoned that Gabriel wouldn't appreciate it. Instead, she leaned back against the log slightly away, a small gesture of distance. "Once the

Matriarchy left the ground behind, they also left quite a few of the prejudices there too. Although you could argue their distrust and dislike for men has become a cultural touchstone for them."

"Them? You do not...share their views?"

Charlotte couldn't help but grin at the edge of hope nibbling at the edge of Gabriel's words. "I do not. Tantric magic is by its nature needful of an entire spectrum of genders, beyond even the simple poles of male and female. Imagine the waves of opposing magnets. Magic is found along the lines of force between them, the attractions, the repulsions. But the Matriarchy does everything in their power to deny the masculine facets. They intentionally hobble the Art with the same backward thinking of the men who would rule them."

"I guessed as much from the rumors," Gabriel said, nodding.

"Oh, please, before I continue, you must entertain me with those," Charlotte laughed.

"Nothing much to tell," Gabriel said, his grin matching hers. "Preachers and priests say you are night devils, sin this, sin that. The same old horseshit they shoveled against my kind, just with altered pronouns and pejoratives. The Bible has passages aplenty for the enslavement of both my people and yours. I wouldn't want to spoil the company by reciting their hateful screeds."

"Fair enough," Charlotte allowed. "Anyway, my wife betrayed me with another lover. We were already the odd ducks out for being mostly monogamous, an embarrassment among tantric practitioners on par with being the loose woman in a congregation. We didn't really have a crew to speak of, so when I kicked her out and took possession of the ship the title of Captain just kind of dropped in on me."

"You never sought to chart your own course?" Gabriel asked.

"Oh, I've always done that," Charlotte chuckled. "But I never wanted to lead, never wanted to be the one that asked the tough questions. I just, sort of, couldn't help myself. I never cared much that I was an outcast among outcasts, and Lauren, my ex, seemed to like that about me. I thought she loved it, and me. But she went behind my back and slept with someone that once shared our bed before her hateful rhetoric made me cut ties."

"Wait," Gabriel put up a hand. "This third woman, she shared a bed with both of you, but your wife cheated with her? How is that possible?"

Charlotte grimaced. "That was rather the thought process of Lauren. Even after I asked her to stop seeing Erin. Even after I begged her. Even after she promised. But she broke that promise. No matter how you judge our morals, surely you can understand how that was crossing a line."

Gabriel threw the stick into the fire. "Yes. Yes, I believe I do. A promise is a promise is a promise. Whether for someone's freedom, or for a pledge of fidelity. You do not break your word. Without your honor, no other possession will ever fill the hole it makes in you."

They sat there in silence, sharing an unspoken bond between them. Charlotte didn't have to ask to know he was talking from experience. The only promise that people seemed able and willing to keep was that of pain, of betrayal. Gabriel's wooden arm and hand were proof enough of that.

Suddenly, a thought occurred to her,

"You said your grandfather's magic started working?" Charlotte asked. "When was this? Twenty years ago?"

Gabriel cocked his head. "That is a rather specific time. But, no, it only began to function a couple years ago. But when it came, the surge was powerful, and it coincided with the formation of the Bright."

"No, that's impossible," Charlotte said, shaking her head. "The Bright has been in place for the last twenty years. And that's when magic re-emerged. Or rather, it's when the tantric Art began working. For some reason, no other form of magic has produced any noticeable results."

"Yes, that explains the troubles I've had," Gabriel nodded, looking down at his repaired arm. "Even the potions and unguents I had made before we were caught by the shimmering border have lost some of their power. I've been on this side of the Bright for nearly three years, and it took an inordinate amount of work to bring about new alchemical concoctions out of local plants and animals. At first, I assumed it was just too different than what I was used to."

"I'm frankly surprised it worked at all," Charlotte said. "But I still don't understand. The Bright has cut us off for nearly twenty years. Not two. Not five."

"What year is it?" Gabriel said, keeping an unreadable expression.

"1856, of course," Charlotte replied. "What are you playing at?"

"The year is 1865 for me. Or rather, it was when we entered the Bright."

Charlotte shook her head, confused.

"Are you saying you're from the future?" she asked.

"Or you are from the past," Gabriel countered. "It's all a matter of perspective, after all. In the end, what is the difference? With our two worlds so completely cut off, what matters the date?"

"But wait a minute," Charlotte objected. "Was there no Bright then in 1863 and earlier? Were people able to travel to Europe?"

"Indeed, they were," Gabriel said. "Although in my timeline there was no sign of aviatrixes and flying cities in 1856, no magic at all. But we had more on our mind than Europeans; the Kansas Wars during that time were fuel that slow-burned eventually into the Civil War."

"There was a war?"

"An inevitability, a cancerous pustule from the very founding of the nation," Gabriel said. "The war was still going strong and bloody when I sailed my stolen Confederate ship into the Bright. I care not to recount it in full, but the Southern states seceded from the rest of the country, cloaking it in the rhetoric of states' rights: mind you, it was specifically the right to own human beings. The North was not content to let them destroy the United States, sundering the nation in two. It was a powder keg waiting for the last spark to ignite."

There was an uncomfortable silence.

"Go ahead, ask," Gabriel sighed.

"Your education level…"

"Is much higher than you expected," he finished. "I sound like a man of learning, not a runaway slave. That is quite intentional. I stole books that sat unread on the shelf of my so-called superior, teaching myself with every scrap of knowledge I could glean. And teaching others, as well. Every word, every letter I learned was paid for in blood. And I would do it all again in an instant. Education opened new worlds to me…although, I did not expect the Bright to make it quite so literal."

There was another leaden lull to the conversation.

"The time difference does make me wonder about the Pacific Bright and what lays beyond it," Gabriel said, breaking the tension. "How far in the future or past is their world? Decades, centuries, … millennia?"

"There's another border further to your west?" Charlotte asked, fascinated.

Gabriel nodded. "Oh, that is right, you would not know. The Pacific Bright runs through the Hawaiian Islands and bisects the ocean. A few men of learning contend there are even more Brights out there, cutting our world up into strange little slices of reality."

"There are rumors of one in the Ural Mountains," Charlotte said softly, thoughts racing each other through her head.

"Rumors?" Gabriel scoffed. "Does not your Matriarchy have control of the skies? I would think the presence of another Bright would warrant your attention."

Charlotte shook her head. "It wasn't exactly prohibited, but the Crones have been busy working Europe and Africa over, trying to elicit change while rescuing who we could.

We don't have any resupply bases out that way. The Ottoman Empire and things east of it were…well, they were largely ignored. Most of the aviatrixes were preoccupied with matters in the old homelands."

Gabriel gestured at the ruins of the ancient Temple of Ishtar. "Or so you were told. Call them Ishtar, Eros, any of the multiple names for the god of love, this is their temple, and their source of power resides within."

"I don't know what you mean," Charlotte said carefully. She'd been so out of practice conversing with those not in the Matriarchy that she realized she might have let too much slip out. Gabriel wasn't using the alchemical grasses anymore, but that didn't mean the man didn't have other ways of eliciting the truth. His eyes were disarmingly kind and understanding, and his cologne was perfectly chosen to complement his natural scent.

"Are you still going to pretend there is no temple full of secrets here?" Gabriel sighed. "Truly? Is this the waltz we must dance?"

Charlotte, not trusting herself to speak, slowly nodded.

Gabriel buried his face in exasperation in his hands.

"Fine," he said, shaking his head. "Then you have forced the issue. I will have the secrets I require, even if the methods are less than ideal. I had hoped to avoid this."

"What are you playing at?" Charlotte asked, concerned.

Gabriel pulled out a pocket watch, checking it. "You will see in…five…four…"

A massive explosion cut him off.

Chapter 3

Smoke blotted out the stars above the Temple of Ishtar, and another explosion sent a plume of fire and dust up again into the night sky.

"A little early," Gabriel said, clicking the watch closed as he rose. "But, still, more punctual than I expected."

"What was that?" Charlotte demanded, standing up in numb shock.

"An explosive ten times as strong as the black powder you Europeans use," Gabriel replied. "Apparently it needed just a touch more, though. The doors must have been stronger than expected. That buffoon is rather lucky that he did not blow himself up with the first batch. It is rather unstable, after all."

Charlotte spun the man around, grabbing the lapels of his jacket. "What did you do, Gabriel?"

He answered with a sly grin. "If you refuse to tell me directly about what you have seen, I have no other option than to press forward with my plans. I was fully willing to send a flare up to stop Jackson from his dirty work. But you made it necessary."

He bent over and hefted his backpack on. Careful not

to move too rapidly he retrieved his cane, making sure that Charlotte was not going to lunge against him.

"Well?" he asked, making a half bow from the weight of the pack, using the cane to take some of the weight. "Shall we go see what you struggled to hide?"

Despite his burden, he was still quick enough that Charlotte had to half-jog to keep up with him as they climbed up the slight ridge separating the camp from the ruins of the temple.

"Where did you see that?" Charlotte demanded in a strained voice, suddenly realizing that she was missing a crucial part of his mystery. "The Engine you are seeking."

Gabriel slowed, his eyes staring blankly into the distance. "It was burnt into my mind. When I was in the Bright. It holds secrets dark and dire, and power untapped."

"That's what you're after? Power?" Charlotte scoffed. "And here I thought you were different than other men."

Gabriel barked a derisive laugh. "You have no idea how different I am. And who does not crave power? Only power, only strength, can change things. The larger the ideal you seek to fight, the more power you need. Anyone who tells you different is only trying to keep the power for himself."

"The world is not as simple as that," Charlotte said, shaking her head.

There was a dour look on Gabriel's face. "That depends on just how much power you have. The stronger you are, the less problems there are. And magic? It is a primal strength, the very basis of all other forces. Everyday magic like electricity, or the more exotic forms like what we practice. It's all power, of one kind or another."

The Temple of Ishtar came into view as they crested the ridge and the dust and smoke cleared from a gentle night breeze. Charlotte had only briefly seen the partially collapsed entrance to the Temple when she had flown in on the *Harlot's Promise*. In the darkness, it appeared that both Jackson and Gabriel hadn't noticed the clear depression in the dirt where the massive slabs of stone had slid apart to reveal the hidden entrance right under their feet. Even now Gabriel was running across and stumbling over the very entrance he was seeking.

Just as Charlotte was murmuring a silent prayer of thanks for the darkness, the morning sun peeked over the desert skyline in the east. The first rays of dawn showed the ground brush and scraggly trees uproot and pushed by the mechanism. But, thankfully, there were other matters distracting Gabriel.

There was a fight in front of the Temple.

Jackson had a broken nose, blood flowing thickly, as he circled, his hands clenched into fists. Rather than Tash, he was facing off against Arslan, the male form of the merged courtesan's body who was also warily pacing, fists raised. Instead of the lovely hourglass form of Tash, Arslan had wide, squared shoulders. He was as bald and hairless as Tash, with gold eyes and perfect porcelain skin, but his jaw was sharp and rugged. The white suit he'd converted from Tash's dress was now drawn tight across his muscular chest, and the pants had been cinched to show off his tight ass rather than Tash's ample bottom.

Behind them the ancient entrance to the Temple of Ishtar smoldered, the stone doors that had sat closed for centuries broken. But there was simply more rubble beyond the destroyed doors; likely as not, all the normal temple above the secret complex had collapsed. The explosive had started several small fires in the undergrowth around the entrance, with black smoke stinging Charlotte's eyes.

They had no idea of the intricate labyrinth of corridors underneath, the true Temple of the mysterious Kurians. And Charlotte had no intention of sharing that particular fact.

"Y'all need to corral your dandy," Jackson spat out. It was hard to tell through the busted lip, but Charlotte was pretty sure he'd lost one of his stained teeth.

"Stop blowing up historical places of worship and I shall stop striking you," Arslan replied, staring at the bigger man like he was a talking cockroach. "Besides, I am not the one bleeding."

"Jackson, stop now," Gabriel commanded.

"Now you just listen here, you—"

Whatever Jackson had been about to say was interrupted by Gabriel raising his prosthetic wooden hand and clenching his fist. Jackson gave a strangled cry and clutched at his chest, falling to his knees. Charlotte felt the power flowing from man to man like a gentle stream, the magic trail leading from one to the other.

"How are you doing that?" she asked.

"It is rather simple," Gabriel responded. "I have replaced several of his internal organs with botanical synthetics. The heart that beats is a vine-tangled mass of moss, and the lungs that breathe are orchid blossoms of darkest violet."

Charlotte gave him a horrified look.

"Save your sanctimony," Gabriel grunted, releasing his fist. Jackson collapsed in the sand, gasping for air like a fish stranded on dry land. "You have no idea what kind of man he is."

Arslan left his opponent in the dirt, straightening his short coat and shirt collar. He turned to Gabriel, and a smile that could dazzle kings and emperors spread across Arslan's immaculate face. Although she much preferred the Tash form of the courtesan, Charlotte mused that if Arslan wasn't gay that he would have certainly taken her breath away.

Charlotte's finely-tuned senses quavered as she took note of Gabriel's sudden intake of air, the blush of blood rushing to his dark face, and the nearly imperceptible shift in his aura. Suddenly, she understood why Arslan had taken control of the body. He'd noticed before her while peeking out of the corner of Tash's mind. Although Gabriel had obviously shown attraction to her, he was having a much stronger reaction to Arslan and his perfect male physique. She'd seen the same dichotomy of behaviors before, many times.

Gabriel was bisexual.

Arslan crossed the distance with a stride that naturally showed off the bulge in his pants as well as his sculpted musculature. Although he'd destroyed Tash's favorite dress to make a set of clothes they'd both be comfortable in, Charlotte had to admit the automaton was a hell of a seamster.

"I..." stammered Gabriel, reaching his hand out to shake. "I do not believe we have, ah, been introduced."

Arslan took the proffered hand; but instead of shaking it he brought it up to his lips and placed a delicate kiss on the back side. Gabriel's face was burning with a mix of emotions that was all too familiar to Charlotte. She wasn't the only Liberty Ship captain to help rescue the less-than-straight from the oppressive regimes of their homeland, but she'd ferried more than her fair share of them to havens. Although no man was ever allowed on Godmother, the Matriarchy took a benign view to gay and bisexual men, and many considered them to be comrades in arms against the abuses of conservative governments and religious persecution. Given what Charlotte knew of the Deep South, there was no doubt in her mind that such a gesture as Arslan had given was virtually unknown to Gabriel.

"I am called Arslan," the automaton said, his voice deeper and more musical than when he'd spoken with Charlotte. She could sense the light touch of magic woven into the words, not enough to overwhelm, but just enough to set the other man at ease.

"My name is Gabriel," he managed to say, although the words tripped over each other.

"I know," Arslan purred. He had not released Gabriel's hand, and the man seemed in no hurry to reclaim it from the automaton's grip. They were locked in a gaze that would have blasted lesser beings to pieces. So much was said in the small exchanges with eyes, and even the featureless gold orbs of Arslan seemed able to communicate desire through them.

"Making me fucking sick," Jackson gasped. He'd managed to get to his knees.

Gabriel didn't look away from Arslan. He merely held his free hand out and clenched it into a fist again. Jackson gave a wordless gasp and fell over once more, clutching his chest.

"Stop that!" Charlotte said, sick to her stomach at what she was seeing. Magic was of life, and to use it to torture was against all the Art stood for.

Gabriel finally managed to break his delightful staring contest with Arslan and spared a withering look for Charlotte.

"Shall I tell you who he really is?" Gabriel asked, his voice as hollow as the haunted look that passed over his face. "Surely once you hear of how he bought and sold my parents, my grandparents, my friends, that will extinguish any pity you have for him. Or shall I regale you about my escape attempts, and the parts of me he took, that which I use plant life to simulate now. Perhaps the tale of how he used me as the abject example of the penalties of disobeying, watched me struggle, laughed at it. Would any of that, perchance, give you pause in your judgments?"

Charlotte shook her head. "No, it wouldn't. He can be the biggest piece of shit in this world, and from your descriptions he is. But to pervert magic to hurt, to harm; that is what turns my stomach like spoiled milk."

"This is not your Art," Gabriel said, pulling his glove off. The deep grain and polished wood of his false hand moved like skin and bone as he spread his fingers wide. "This is not my grandfather's magic either. I managed to merge the wisdom of the old with the knowledge of the present, creating an alchemy never seen before. Even now, in a land drained of magic, mine still works."

Arslan shared a puzzled look with Charlotte.

"Drained?" the courtesan asked, trying to get Gabriel's attention back on him. The dark-skinned man turned, his eyes softening from the righteous rage he'd begun building in word and thought.

"As dry as this desert," Gabriel said. His expression mellowed more as he stared into the auric gaze of Arslan. "Somehow your Matriarchy has captured the lifeblood of these lands, the magic, and left no water at the well for anyone else."

Charlotte thought about the big batteries she had within the *Harlot's Promise*. They carried an impressive charge that, when fully juiced, could keep the ship flying for weeks without refueling. Godmother, the sentient flying city of the Matriarchy, had innumerable such batteries, banks and banks of them, some the size of small ships. She'd never considered that they were storing more than just the mystic forces generated in the city itself.

The Matriarchy had long held the public opinion that only their form of magic worked, that all other practitioners, especially males, were pretenders to the throne, charlatans and fakes. But if they'd used Godmother to absorb all the ambient magic from the land that would explain why there had arisen no other practitioners on the ground. The constant back and forth of the floating city over Europe and Africa would have been to vacuum up the energies, not to escape the fixed artillery each land had used to try and down them. The Matriarchy had created the problem and then acted as if the problem itself validated their superiority.

Still, there was no way to tell if Gabriel was telling the truth. He had just as much reason to lie as anyone else, perhaps more so as he was a stranger in a strange land. Just because the ideas he proposed made sense didn't mean they were correct. Charlotte had come a long way since she believed in the inherent virtue of the sisterhood she'd spent her entire adult life in. But to think that they'd denied magic to everyone else while hypocritically stealing it out from under them? That was a bridge slightly too far, even for an outcast rebel from the Matriarchy.

The light of morning blazed hot and bright, dispelling the shadows and the morning dew as the sun rose higher over the ridge. Gabriel put up a hand to shield his eyes as the sunlight picked out the silver runes embedded in Arslan's alabaster skin, making the gold and ivory automaton glitter in a spectacular display. The momentary distraction from the object of his fascination let the alchemist's gaze wander, and his eyes widened as he finally took note of the disturbed detritus of the uprooted bushes and trees that marked the massive entrance slabs underfoot. Arslan tried to bring his attention back unsuccessfully as the small man covered the ground quickly, tracing the outline of the trapdoors with his eyes and muttered calculations. Charlotte knew it was pointless to try more distractions; she'd felt that discovery spark before, that pure joy at a solution to a problem you'd long tried to solve. Even Arslan's stunning beauty was forgotten at that moment.

While Gabriel had been distracted, the disheveled

Jackson had regained his footing, shooting sullen looks at the group. The big dirty man couldn't seem to decide who he hated more, so he settled on a loathing gaze directed at everyone. He moved toward his own pack, dropped in the scuffle with Arslan. The automaton had interrupted him planting more explosives and the tightly wrapped white paper sticks were spilling out of his bag. Charlotte shuddered as she imagined the sheer explosive force they were capable of generating.

"Be careful with those," she told Jackson.

He just sneered at her. But the man seemed lost on what to do next. He hadn't recognized the hidden slabs that opened into the cavern; he still thought it was his job to blast through the rubble into the Temple of Ishtar. But the cave-ins were just more boulders and dirt, and Charlotte could see him trying to guess how much would be needed. Since the entire top floor was nothing but rubble and ruins, he'd be blasting for quite a while.

Gabriel, however, was much closer to a real answer. He was on his hands and knees, scrabbling around in the dirt atop the massive hidden slabs. Arslan tried to engage with him again, but the alchemist was more interested in the mystery and his end goal than flirting with the mechanical man.

"But how does it open?" Gabriel muttered, perplexed by the lack of any sort of switches.

His eyes had taken on a blazing quality, as if the nearness of discovery was taunting him, tempting him. Charlotte was trying not to gain his attention, and waved Arslan off. But it only took a few minutes for his gaze to settle on the Doll and the aviatrix. Charlotte steeled herself for the inevitable tirade of questions, accusations, and threats.

But Gabriel was not that kind of man.

"You know this secret, don't you?" he asked, his tone gentle. He gave a heavy sigh. "Let me guess. No man is to enter. You'll die before telling me. How dare I seek to violate the sanctity of this place."

Charlotte was startled by his calm demeanor. "Pretty much, yeah, all that. Let me ask you a question: why is this Engine of Eros so important to you? You said you witnessed it in the Bright, but so what? Why go to all this trouble?"

"Power," Gabriel answered with a shrug. "The answer is the same as before. I need its power. I have used hook and crook for three years to search for it."

"But to what end?" Charlotte pressed. "Power is all well and good, but the directing of it, the utilization, is what defines a person."

"True enough," Gabriel replied. "Allow me to ask you this, Captain Frost. What is the purpose of those airships your Matriarchy use?"

"The answer is in the name," Charlotte said. "Liberty Ships are freedom to their crews and represent a new life for those we can rescue from the ground."

"If only such a thing existed in the Deep South," Gabriel said, slowly and deliberately choosing his words. "If such a system of ships and captains could be deployed, imagine all the suffering, all the pain and humiliation, that such a fleet could stave off. That's what I seek, and why I seek it. The Engines of Eros contains enough power to launch a second flying city, a Godfather if you will. A sanctuary. Why is it only your people, your countries of origin, who deserve to be saved from awful fates?"

Charlotte didn't have an immediate, easy answer for him. She'd studied her history, and the other side of the Atlantic held crimes and horrors aplenty for those of darker skin tones. Gabriel was a living testament to the barbarity that his people endured daily. What right did she have, Charlotte asked herself, to deny liberation to such a downtrodden people?

"There's one problem with your quest," she said, suddenly realizing why he made her uneasy. "You use magic to hurt, to harm. Would you be content to just liberate your people, or would you extract a measure of vengeance against those who have wronged you and yours? Jackson is a result of your choices. It wasn't enough to kill him, was it? You had to exert control over him, crush him under the same wheel that crushed you."

Gabriel spread his hands and shrugged. "You can say you would choose differently; but would you really? Can you fathom the evils this sniveling coward has been party to?"

"No," Charlotte said, shaking her head. "I can try to imagine, but I have not endured the Hell that you have. But isn't that the chance to be better?"

"An eye for an eye leaves the world blind," Arslan said, moving between the captain and the alchemist. "Look at me, Gabriel. Am I the product of love, or of hate?"

Gabriel shook his head, unconvinced. "You are the product of a dream, of that there is no doubt. But how can a people dream when they are caught in a nightmare?"

Arslan stepped closer, raising his hand and gently stroking Gabriel's cheek. "People need dreams most when there is naught but nightmares around," Arslan said.

Gabriel couldn't help himself and leaned his jaw into the touch in a feline motion, luxuriating in it. But after a moment he shook himself, like he'd forced reality back in, and drew his head back from the embrace.

"Pretty words," Gabriel sighed. "But will they free my people? Will they reunite families torn asunder by Jackson and his ilk?"

"I cannot tell you the future; only that the present is here, now," Arslan said, reaching out once more to soothe Gabriel. The alchemist shrank back, but Arslan left his hand out, beseeching. "Captain Frost is correct to deny you. Although your cause is just, there is a cruelty in you to inflict such a state on this beast of a man."

"Shall I just kill him then and call it done?" Gabriel growled, swatting Arslan's hand away. "Is that the correct way? Would you judge me less cruel to have him strung up by a rope, as so many of mine have been?"

"There aren't any easy answers," Charlotte admitted. "But that doesn't mean we give up. We keep searching, reaching, trying to be better than we were yesterday. It's the only way to have hope for tomorrow."

"Hope!" Gabriel spat, getting angrier. "What right have you to use the word, when you stand there, free and whole? Do you preach to my people now like the Christian pastors who thump a bible in one hand while they hold the chain in the other, teaching us that slavery is our proper place both now and in the hereafter?"

Charlotte stood mute. There was nothing she could say that would make things easier on the alchemist. Their words had inflamed the situation, bringing Gabriel's temper to a boil they had not expected. Arslan shook his head sadly.

"Tell me how to access this damned Temple!" Gabriel demanded in a shout, his face flushed with anger. "If you have an ounce of decency in you, give me the tools to end the war and save my people!"

Charlotte's heart ached, but she stayed silent. As just as Gabriel's cause was, he had demonstrated that he had no compunction about using magic to cause suffering. He'd given in to the pain in himself, feeding it by inflicting that horror on another. Charlotte had no doubt that the greasy Jackson deserved his fate; but Gabriel had not just stopped him, not just killed him. He had enslaved the slaver. Rather than rebuke the sin, he had taken it into himself, given it a spot in his heart. There was no doubt in Charlotte's mind.

Gabriel could not be allowed to acquire an Engine of Eros.

Arslan let his hand drop, knowing that the angry man would not take it. There was a sadness in his features, deeper than just not being able to connect with Gabriel. Arslan was thinking of his own lost love, his Kudurri, and what he'd do to bring him back. Perhaps he held some understanding of what drove the alchemist. Love, whether for an individual or for a group of people, was a powerful force, a motivator beyond compare. The problem was that it could also blind you, both to your own faults and pitfalls in your reasoning. It was all too easy to excuse horrific behavior in the name of love and justice.

Snapping out of his reverie, Arslan's head jerked up. He seemed to have noticed something in the sky. His auric gaze was obviously tracking an object that Charlotte couldn't see, so she pulled her spyglass from the belt and extended it. Sweeping the western horizon, she noticed the glint that had attracted Arslan's attention. It was moving rapidly across the sky in a smooth fashion, canvas sails fluttering like insect wings from its tiny wood and steel body.

"Shit," Charlotte muttered. "Arslan, is that what I think it is?"

The automaton nodded. "I believe so. One of Godmother's Enforcers. Heading straight toward us."

Gabriel and Jackson cupped their hands over their eyes, scanning the sky.

"What are you talking about?" Gabriel asked.

"Enforcers are remote-controlled drones," Charlotte explained, clicking her spyglass closed to hang on her belt again. "There's only one thing that can mean.

"The Matriarchy has found us."

Chapter 4

"Lilith's tit," Charlotte swore. "We've got to get to cover before the flitter sees us. Luckily, no one has recently used explosives to send up a plume of black smoke directly marking our location. Oh, wait, no. We're fucked."

Jackson looked confused, but Gabriel shook his head.

"You are the soul of subtlety," he groused. "I take it you are not on good terms with your Matriarchy right now."

"That's one way of putting it," Charlotte said. "All I did was spirit their prize automaton away, shoot down a few Enforcer drones, and uncover a secret they killed to keep for two decades. You'd be forgiven for assuming they were cross with me."

"I suppose that leaves only one option, then," Gabriel grinned. He stomped his foot on the hidden slab that led into the cavern. "Open sesame."

Charlotte sighed heavily. She shared a look with Arslan, who slightly shook his head.

"We cannot," he objected.

"No choice, thanks to the smoke," Charlotte said with a shrug. "There's zero chance that they don't come looking at the Temple after the explosions."

"It would be a sacrilege to give this one even a step inside," Arslan objected, pointing at Jackson. "We can hide. We can run."

"Hide where?" Charlotte asked with a note of panic in her voice, sweeping her arm across the barren landscape. "Are we going to pretend to be scrub brush? I'd wager none of us are experts at desert camouflage. And running? The *Harlot's Promise* is unable to even lift off. So we go on foot, through the desert, with flyers at our backs? All we'd do is die tired."

Gabriel made no pretense at hiding his joy. The only one who didn't understand the conversation was ironically the biggest sticking point: Jackson. Neither the aviatrix nor the courtesan wanted to give access to the Temple to such a man. It felt like his very presence would pollute the place and leave a lasting stain. But Charlotte was not content to let him perish by being the only one left out. She hated doing it, but there was no other way.

"Arslan…" she started.

"No!" he practically yelled. "I refuse. Better to take our chances out here than to let that…'man'…into the Temple."

"Please don't make me do this," Charlotte said, shaking her head. "You know I can make it an order."

Arslan's perfect face held an enraged visage. "You would not."

"We don't have time for this," Gabriel interrupted. He'd taken a small root out and chewed it, which turned his eyes a startling shade of blue. Where before he'd scanned the horizon to no avail, it was easy to see he was now tracking the Enforcer drone by sight. "That flitter of yours has changed course, doubling back on itself. I'd imagine there are already several of your Liberty Ships on the way."

"He's right," Charlotte sighed. "As much as I hate this…Arslan, I order you to—"

"Backstabbing bitch," Arslan muttered.

Charlotte paused for a long moment, then shook her head with an exasperated sigh. "You're right: I can't do this and look at myself in the mirror. I'm many things, but a hypocrite isn't one of them."

Arslan sputtered in genuine surprise.

"You're not going to command me to reveal the Temple?"

"No, I'm not," Charlotte said. "But it doesn't change the fact that we have incoming Matriarchy ships. You know it all too well. We stay out here, we're begging to be captured."

Arslan blew out an irritated sigh, his golden eyes rolling. "At least leave behind the cur."

"We cannot," Gabriel piped up. "He would sell us out in a heartbeat, assuming that he didn't say something so offensive they'd gun him down where he stood."

"Then why do you travel with him?" Charlotte asked. "Why keep such a low being at your side?"

Gabriel stood mute, offering no reasons that he, a well-heeled gentleman in appearance and manners, would travel with such a beast.

"I'm standing right here, missy," Jackson growled. He'd straightened up to his full height, clenching grimy fists as if imagining throttling the aviatrix. "You don't disrespect me and get to stand there with all your teeth."

Several things happened in the span of a breath. Jackson lunged for Charlotte as Gabriel raised his hand and tightened it into a fist. Whereas Tash would have leapt to her defense, Arslan contented himself by sticking out a leg, tripping Jackson. The big man went down with a throttled scream, his body reacting to the mystic command from Gabriel.

"Does he do any other tricks than writhe?" Arslan asked dryly, flicking off an imaginary spot from his coat sleeves and straightening them.

"A couple," Gabriel replied, walking up to Jackson, who had curled into the fetal position. With no hint of mercy or hesitation Gabriel kicked Jackson squarely in the ribs. The big man cried out.

"That's enough of that!" Charlotte said, intervening and pushing Gabriel back. "He might be an asshole, but kicking a man when he's down and helpless is low."

Gabriel's expression looked haunted for a moment. "You have no idea how much pain this bastard deserves."

Before Charlotte could respond, a deep melodramatic sigh interrupted them.

"Fine," Arslan said, stretching the word. "I'll open the way. But I still think we should just leave them out here to distract the Matriarchy. If this goes bad, if that louse breaks anything, I'm holding you responsible, Captain Frost."

Charlotte snorted. "Afraid he'll break an Enkidu? I doubt he's got what it takes."

Arslan shook his head. "There are delicate balances

within the Temple of Ishtar. You, of all people, should realize that."

The clockwork man led the motley group down a small incline a hundred yards to a seemingly normal pile of rocks. He shot a venomous look at Jackson as he reached out and twisted a rock under an overhang.

There was a deep grinding noise in the pile of rocks, and they shifted as a door opened into the secret tunnels under the ruins. The air was cooler than the desert morning, and Charlotte idly wondered if she could copy the environmental magics the Kurians used for her ship. She shook her head to clear it of such unimportant notions, stepping on to the inclined floor.

There was a whooshing sound behind Charlotte, and she turned to see that Arslan was transforming into Tash before the shocked eyes of Gabriel and Jackson. Her hips widened as her shoulders narrowed, and all the welcome curves that could tempt a holy man filled out the white and yellow suit as clips became undone in the fabric.

"He's that pissed at me, huh?" Charlotte asked.

"Arslan is not the only one unhappy with your choice," Tash answered, unusually icy in her demeanor.

"We didn't have a choice," Charlotte said. "The drone—"

"Is a respectable distance from Godmother," Tash interrupted. "We have no idea how far behind reinforcements are. There was time for another option."

"What option?" Charlotte nearly shouted, frustrated at both the forms of the courtesan. "The *Harlot's Promise* is so damaged it can barely fly, even if it wasn't completely drained by the sapping field. We can't run, we can't hide. The best we can do is lock ourselves in the Temple and hope we can figure out some way to prevent their access."

Gabriel was pushing them to proceed into the Temple, his face lit up like a schoolboy with his first kiss. The alchemist ran his fingers over the softly glowing, blue-glazed walls with alien script dancing behind them. He gasped in amazement at the twin Enkidu guarding the passage. The monstrous machines were as large as horses, with four legs that ended in multi-fingered hands. Their ivory plates were segmented like an insect's, with golden gearwork underneath. A giant scorpion-like tail curved over their backs, but instead of a stinger it had a multi-pronged tool. With a head that flared from a pyramidal eyeless face into wide plates they could have been mistaken for manticores of legend in the night. When they alighted from the incline and saw the army of Enkidu through the glass floor of the complex they were stunned by the sight, nervously stepping on the glass as if afraid to shatter it with their weight.

Charlotte came to a T-section where the path split.

"Do not," warned Tash. "There is still a choice to make. Please."

The aviatrix didn't bother answering and turned down the path that led to the Temple's power and control center. She could have wasted hours getting Gabriel and Jackson lost in the complex, but that would just burn precious time. Charlotte could feel the weight of the Matriarchy's impending arrival, gnawing at her gut like a parasite.

Tash began moving faster than the humans, her feet

gliding on the smooth floor like an ice skater over a pond. She showed no desire to remain behind with them, and Charlotte could feel the distance stretch out between them as an emotional gulf. She'd ignored the Doll's warnings, and it wasn't sitting well with the automaton. Tash was beautiful and intelligent, but Charlotte knew the Matriarchy and, more importantly, Godmother, would be upon them soon. Or Ereshkigal, to call her the Kurian name. Whatever name the entity preferred, she'd played the long con on Charlotte, taking a young girl's trust, and becoming the only stable confidant in her life. The aviatrix wasn't sure how she should feel about it, but there was a chasm of betrayal that yawned under her, a bottomless pit of benighted shame. Instead of the rightful rage that she imagined she'd be feeling, there was just a sick uncertainty and anchorless miasma. It was like finding out your parents had lied to you your entire life.

And what had been Ereshkigal's plan? Why did she even bother with Charlotte? A sick fascination with manipulating humans? There were plenty of those in the Amethyst City. And nearly as many who were more pliable, more likely to bend to the intelligence's will. If anything, Godmother's guidance in Charlotte's life had created a more rebellious, more independent version of the aviatrix. What game could Ereshkigal be playing at?

Regardless of the answer to that question, Charlotte was sure of one thing: once Godmother knew that the Temple had been breached, she'd act. The secret had been kept for twenty years; dozens of aviatrixes had been killed to shut down the facility. That kind of coverup being blown open would bring a severe response from the entity that had manipulated the Matriarchy for its entire life. That the rebellious daughter was behind it would only hasten the answering investigation, not stymie it.

The Enforcer flitter was proof positive that Godmother wasn't willing to lose either Charlotte or Tash so easily. Although there was no telling how far behind would be the Legion of Lilith ships, there was no doubt they were coming. They'd have little trouble commandeering some of the more militant Liberty Ships, and the fact the Legion had been constructing their own for some time was the worst-kept secret in the city.

The group entered the power control room, the beating heart of the Temple complex. Banks of various gems glittered around the perimeter of the room, rubies, sapphires, and emeralds suspended in a strange black liquid. The center of the room was taken up by three pillars made of the same gold alloy as Tash's internal mechanisms, ten feet in circumference, each in a different state of disrepair. The first was missing most of its data diamonds and was likely what remained of Ereshkigal's prison. The second was burnt and twisted, most of it having melted under some intense heat. The third one was intact, with all its gems, but they were dark and lifeless. Tash was already at the blank wall that ran the length of the chamber, hands clasped behind her back, facing away from the group. That she looked like a servant awaiting command did not escape Charlotte's notice. There was a rigidity of stance that she hated.

Shamhat was still communing with her broken pillar,

but upon Charlotte's entry the jury-rigged frame hopped off the column and skittered toward the aviatrix.

Jackson screamed and cursed as the small insectile automaton tapped her way across the glass floor. To his credit Gabriel kept a cool head, but even he appeared to be disconcerted by Shamhat, holding his cane out like he was going to stab her.

"That's a Kiki frame," Charlotte said by way of explanation. "I adapted it from the tail of an Enkidu, the large mechanical sentries that we passed. It houses an ally."

Shamhat leapt for the aviatrix, and Gabriel reflexively swung his cane. The automaton twisted in the air, avoiding the clumsy blow with impossible grace before landing on Charlotte's front. Although she should have weighed over a hundred pounds, the Kiki frame utilized the same mass-negating magic that both the Enkidu and the Matriarchy's airships used to slip the surly bonds of gravity. Shamhat skittered around to Charlotte's back before molding herself to the aviatrix, folding her six golden legs around the captain's midriff and forming an alabaster and gold corset. The recessed head of the frame extended, looking over Charlotte's shoulder. The fae lights that had been used as her eyes glowed a steady yellow, with occasional orange flashes.

"What th' hell is that thang?" Jackson spat, reaching inside his pack for one of the alchemical explosives.

"This is Shamhat," Charlotte said with a shrug. "She runs this place. Or at least she used to, a long time ago."

Gabriel had a puzzled look on his face as he let his heavy backpack slide down to the floor off his shoulder.

"Enkidu? Shamhat? Are we going to see Gilgamesh strolling through the door next?"

Charlotte remembered someone using the Gilgamesh moniker earlier, but she couldn't quite put her finger on who or when. "You know these names?"

"Any student of the classics would," laughed Gabriel. "Gilgamesh's search for immortality is one of the earliest stories humans created. He had a friend, Enkidu, a wild savage that Gilgamesh was only able to best after a sacred prostitute named Shamhat lay with him."

The aviatrix grew excited. "Does the name 'Ereshkigal' or 'Kurian' mean anything to you?"

"Hmm," Gabriel mused, scratching his chin. He was having trouble concentrating with the object of his three-year quest so close at hand, but he was trying to maintain civility. "I do not know about Kurian specifically, but I believe Kur was the Mesopotamian underworld, their land of the dead. Ereshkigal was the queen of the afterlife."

"Arslan says humans have always told stories about his people," Tash said, still facing away from the group. "Over time the legends evolve into parables and myth."

Charlotte cocked her head to the side. "Are we on speaking terms again, then?"

Tash was still rigid in posture and refused to turn around. "You can order me to converse at any time."

"Damn it, Tash, that's not what I meant, and you know it," Charlotte said with an exasperated sigh.

Shamhat sent miniscule vibrations through Charlotte's body, just enough so that her eardrums would hear the warden's words.

Explain: presence of two foreign humans.

"The Matriarchy is coming for us," Charlotte said, and the fae lights flashed red in anger.

Activate: Enkidu defense protocols.

"I'd love to," Charlotte said to her mechanical corset. "But wasn't that your job?"

Gabriel was looking at the aviatrix like she'd lost her mind.

"I can hear the Kiki frame through our bodily contact," Charlotte explained. "She is distrustful of you, but that's nothing compared to her feelings on the Matriarchy."

Data core: damaged by long-term exposure to suppression field. Unable: activate Enkidu. Suggestion: utilize Kurian-type frame.

"Is there really no other way?" Charlotte asked.

"She is telling you to use me, is she not?" Tash asked, still rigid, still not looking. "If she was able to activate the sentries on her own, I suspect we would not be standing here."

"How did—"

"It is only logical," Tash interrupted.

She raised her hand, extending the innumerable tiny gold barbs from her palm before placing it against the glowing blue wall. Waves of purple emanated out from the contact point. There was a cracking sound, like a frozen lake in the winter, and a sense of a great shift in the Temple.

"Power levels at two percent," Tash said woodenly. Then she made a confused sound. "There is plenty of energy available in the Ishtar engine core. But it is in hibernation mode."

Affirmative: Kurian overseer unresponsive since Matriarchy betrayal.

"Can you wake them up?" Charlotte asked. "We could use their help. If nothing else, I can ask them to start repairs on the *Harlot's Promise*."

Irrelevant: basic repair routines and charging cycle done in sixty-six seconds.

"What?" Charlotte said, shocked. At Tash's odd look she explained.

"Shamhat appears to be telling the truth," Tash said, moving her hands over the wall screen. "I have confirmed the activation of an Enkidu tasked with repairs several hours ago. It appears to coincide with the beginning of Shamhat climbing onto her old engine pillar. The *Harlot's Promise* is ready to launch at your command, Captain."

Clarification: ship repaired to extent of Enkidu capabilities. Libidium frame cracked beyond conventional means of repair. Likelihood of airship destruction upon launch: 13.6%. Likelihood of total airship destruction increases exponentially per 3.2 hour increments.

"Still better than a one hundred percent chance of getting caught with our pants down by the Matriarchy," Charlotte said, impressed. "Thank you, Shamhat. Your initiative is probably going to save our lives."

Gratitude: unnecessary. Repair of airship: needed to tempt Charlotte Frost away from temple and secrets. Reminder: evaluation of Charlotte honesty and Matriarchy ties ongoing.

"At least you're straightforward about wanting to get rid of me," Charlotte laughed softly.

She explained what Shamhat had told her, but Gabriel

was too fascinated by the inactive Eros Engines to pay her much heed. The alchemist had been starry-eyed ever since entering the hidden temple complex, but with the object of his search for the last few years in front of him there was little that could distract him.

He walked around the Ishtar engine, his keen eyes taking note of every detail. The data diamonds refracted his image in their facets, a thousand tiny mirrors cleaved at such an exacting level no human jeweler could have dreamt of. Gabriel was like a man savoring a fine meal, first letting his gaze get its fill, before reaching out his cane to prod one of the diamonds held in place by the metal pillar. Charlotte didn't stop him, interested in what reaction, if any, the engine would have to him.

The golden sheen of the pillar rippled like quicksilver from the diamond he'd touched, sending tiny waves over the entire surface. Charlotte let out a breath in surprise. She'd thought the pillar mounted between ceiling and floor to be solid, with the data gems held in stasis within the golden obelisk. To discover that the medium was liquid simply amazed her.

She turned to Shamhat's broken pillar, the blackened edges of the exploded engine that had once housed the warden sprite of the temple. Hesitantly she reached out to touch it. Instead of liquid, she found the metal to be solid with a fine sheen in the undamaged parts, like steel. Turning to the third pillar, the one missing most of its diamonds, she reached out. Solid, not liquid.

"Shamhat, why did they leave some of Ereshkigal's data

diamonds here? Isn't that like leaving part of your mind behind?" Charlotte asked.

Analogy: correct. Abandonment of diamonds: necessitated by Shamhat's pursuit.

Charlotte nodded. "It's why they rigged the suppression field. They knew you'd come after them, after your prisoner. What lies must Godmother have told them to hoodwink the first aviatrixes. But why didn't you awaken Ishtar to help you? Surely the two of you together would have had enough strength to mobilize the Enkidu army stored below. Isn't that precisely why you have them?"

"I believe I can answer that, with Arslan's whispered help," Tash said, scanning the screen and flicking datasets like a horse swatting at flies. "If I am reading this correctly, the Matriarchy also managed to disrupt Shamhat's access to Ishtar. Some sort of forced hibernation."

Supposition: correct.

"She will be coming back for them," Gabriel suddenly interjected. He'd wandered over to the mostly-empty gold pillar with the Ereshkigal gems. "She left part of her essence here. Until these are back in her possession, this intelligence will never be complete. To what lengths would you go to recover a vital part of yourself that you had lost?"

That he was speaking from experience was not lost on Charlotte.

"Okay, so we need to get Ishtar to wake up," she said, stroking her chin in thought. "A jolt of energy? Could we use alchemy or the tantric Art?"

"Possibly," Tash allowed, but her brow furrowed with worry. "Unfortunately, we have not the time to experiment."

The bottom of Charlotte's stomach felt like it fell out, leaving acidic worry. "Let me guess."

Tash nodded at the obvious. "We have three airships inbound at high speed. At the edge of the sense-net I can feel something huge following them, like the shadow of a mountain. There is little doubt about what it is.

"Godmother is coming to claim the rest of her mind."

Chapter 5

"Then we fight."

Gabriel's voice was firm and unrelenting, and he'd apparently shaken his daze at finding the mythical Engines of Eros. But Charlotte shook her head before Tash and Shamhat could object.

"Even if I was willing to use violence, we're laughably outnumbered," Charlotte said. "The *Harlot's Promise* is in no shape for a fight, and there's no way to activate the Enkidu stored below. That Shamhat managed to activate one to repair my ship is a minor miracle unto itself."

"That is...not quite correct," Tash said, pulling her hands off the wall screen and turning. "There exists a way to activate the Enkidu army for a limited time using the energy left in Shamhat's shattered engine pillar."

"Then let's do that!" Charlotte exclaimed with relief. "Damn it, sugar, you can't just let me sweat like that when you've got the answer right at your fingertips."

Warning: the Tash-Kurian omits salient details.

Charlotte pinched the bridge of her nose and closed her eyes in frustration.

"Okay," she sighed, finally opening her eyes again. "Tell me why it won't work."

Despite their recent quarrel, Tash looked apologetic.

"They would be uncontrolled, little better than beasts off their leash," she explained. "Without Shamhat or Ishtar directing them, they would attack anything they encountered, whether friend or foe."

"So, we fly away and let the army loose to guard the place. That doesn't sound so bad," Charlotte said hopefully. But Tash shook her head.

"They would have a short lifespan," Tash explained. "An hour, maybe two at most, and then they would power down, leaving the temple unguarded once more. All the Matriarchy forces must do is to wait them out. And then they will capture the slumbering Ishtar and restore Ereshkigal's full mind and powers."

"You cannot let them pilfer the Engines!" Gabriel exclaimed. He gestured at the engines. "The almost unfathomable mysteries of these machines, the beauty of them, and, yes, the power they contain. Surely keeping the goddess Ishtar out of their grasp is worth sacrifice."

Charlotte sighed. "Look, we can't fight them. We're lucky Shamhat started repairing and refueling the *Harlot's Promise* when she did. We have an escape option. What do you want us to do, die defending the temple against the Matriarchy and the Legion?"

Gabriel looked like he was on the edge of tears of frustration.

Recommendation: disengage Ishtar's Engine and transport

it to Charlotte-captain's airship along with Ereshkigal's
remaining data diamonds.

"Wait, we can do that?" Charlotte asked, quickly relaying Shamhat's suggestion to the others.

Jackson snorted derisively. "Y'all crazy. That thang must weigh ten tons."

The intact Engine did look like far too much for anyone to move. Even with the lightweight gold alloy, the sheer size of it indicated a weight heavier than any of them could manage. And whatever was holding its liquid in place might suddenly give out if they attempted to move it.

Enkidu: installed unit. Enkidu: can transport it.

"Tash, can you re-task the Enkidu that was working on the *Harlot's Promise*? It should have enough power regardless of when we spin the others up to make it here and back again, right?" Charlotte said.

The Doll turned and placed her hands on the screen wall. Purple flashes shot out like lightning from the contact point, and Tash turned her head to Charlotte to nod assent.

"There still remains one problem," Tash said, worry creasing her perfect brow. "According to what I am reading in this data block the Enkidu is only capable of transporting the Engine after it has been disengaged from the temple systems."

Charlotte felt like a cat leaping at a patch of light only to find her paws empty. She gave a deep sigh and asked the question. "How, then, do we unhook Ishtar from their temple? I suppose it is not as simple as a really big wrench?"

Tash smiled, mischievousness lighting her features. "No...mistress. The coin of the realm is what we need. To make anything happen in the temple of the deity of love, one must pay a most wonderful toll."

The aviatrix's grin mirrored the Doll's. But their mutual excitement was spoiled by a leering Jackson, who slapped his hands together and rubbed them. The slave master thought he was going to get a show.

"Gabriel," Charlotte purred with a hint of menace to it. "Would you be a dear and make sure that disgusting thing stays in the hallway, please?"

Before he could answer, Tash interjected. "No, mistress. We need him."

At Charlotte's horrified look, Tash tittered a laugh.

"I meant we need Gabriel," she said through a giggle. "I am sure that between the Enkidu guarding the door and an unspeakable horror visited upon him by Gabriel that Jackson will have the good sense to stay away from this room."

The color drained from the ruddy man's face at the threat. Gabriel tapped his cane once upon the floor, loudly, making Jackson jump. The older man shuffled out of the room, obviously loath to leave the scene of an orgy in the making. Charlotte shuddered; it was going to take more than a few minutes of foreplay to forget about the creeper in the hall.

A clanking sound outside the room announced the arrival of the active Enkidu, and weak protests from the hall informed them that Jackson was being bodily moved down the corridor away from the lusty participants.

Tash stepped away from the wall screen, letting it return to its neutral white. "There is one other problem. At least for me. The temple has a surfeit of female-pole energy; even before you seduced Shamhat, the echoes of the energy the Matriarchy generated is still present."

A pang of sudden guilt stabbed Charlotte. "Oh, sugar, I'm sorry, I completely forgot that in the heat of the moment—"

Tash held up her hand to forestall the apology. "Mistress, I am not jealous of others spending time with you. I understand full well the needs of the tantric Art, and of the dire situation you found yourself in. Even if I did not, it was needful at the time to save both your life and mine."

"I just don't want you to feel like I did," Charlotte said softly.

"With Lauren," Tash finished, nodding. "That can never be, my sweet captain. For I know full well the difference between the mechanics of sex, and the heart of it. Your body is yours to do with as you will, without anyone's interference."

The Doll placed her hand between Charlotte's breasts. The surprising warmth of the magically-animated ivory and gold throbbed in time to the aviatrix's heartbeat.

"Besides," Tash whispered, drawing Charlotte into an embrace. "I have a piece of you that no one else does, that no one else touches. And you have the same from me."

Charlotte's face flushed brighter than any sexual act could elicit, and her heartbeat was loud in her ears.

"Tash," she whispered, cupping the Doll's face in her hand. "I want...I mean, you know that..."

"Shh," Tash murmured, giving little kisses to the

aviatrix's fingertips. "I know. We have all the time in the world to say it to each other."

Tash stepped away, a wistful longing on her face. "But my sweet mistress, I am not the one called for here," she said. "You need an infusion of male-dominant tantric energy to release the locking mechanisms."

Charlotte couldn't help but give a small mewl of need and frustration as Tash's face started to change, growing heavier and sharper. Shoulders filled out and so did height as buttocks and breasts drew in and hardened into masculine lines. Within only a few seconds Arslan had replaced his female counterpart.

"Intriguing," Gabriel whispered, drawing Charlotte's attention to him. She gave a small laugh; the aviatrix didn't think the miracle of Arslan Tash's transformation would ever fail to impress, even the second time around.

"Why, thank you, handsome," Arslan rumbled, threading magic into the words. "You're not so bad yourself."

Gabriel's dark face turned a shade darker as he blushed, a grin breaking through its restraints. Arslan used the same floor gliding technique that Tash had, but instead of zooming around the room he did a stylish slide up to Gabriel's side, a hungry smile on his face. The flustered alchemist didn't know quite how to react as Arslan took his gloved hand and brought it up.

"This little piggy went to market," Arslan said, pulling on one of the fingers to loosen the glove. "This little piggy dropped his trousers, and this one had the time of his life."

With a flourish Arslan pulled the glove off entirely, and

Gabriel's thoughts were obviously in a place of being disrobed with similar abandon. Arslan slowly and deliberately brought the wooden hand up and kissed it, taking note of the alchemist's flushed reaction.

"So, you do feel it as you would skin," Arslan cooed. "Then, my dear friend, let us see just how much I can do with only a hand."

Charlotte was feeling like a third wheel, and she turned to leave.

"Wait," Gabriel said, his voice as flushed as his face. "I...can you stay?"

The aviatrix looked at Arslan with an arched eyebrow. She and he had been at loggerheads more often than not, and she'd made a vow to him after using the Art to replicate his lover that she wouldn't do that again. But instead of shooting her a dirty look, the automaton merely shrugged his shoulders.

"This isn't a spectator sport," Charlotte said softly. "Do you know of what you ask?"

The excited look came back to Gabriel's face, and he shook his head as he took off his glasses and put them into a safe area where they wouldn't get broken. "Not really. But that too has its own allure. Please. Stay. Help me."

Arslan simply tilted his head in a way that indicated he had no objections.

Charlotte crossed over to where Arslan was peppering light kisses on Gabriel's wooden hand and offered her hand to the alchemist's free one. Gabriel looked grateful as he took her hand in his, luxuriating for a moment in the simple contact. His skin was rough from years of work, both physical and mystical, but there was a comfort in that. The strong grip was still gentle, and Charlotte marveled at the difference between his skin's texture and Tash's. It had been years since Charlotte and Lauren had last availed themselves of a man, and the hunger, the need, suddenly rose in the aviatrix like a coiled serpent.

She spun herself into his arm, taking Gabriel by surprise as her face came to rest next to his with the tight embrace. Charlotte took the initiative, going in for a kiss that was eagerly returned.

Gabriel moaned into the kiss as Arslan licked the alchemist's finger before slowly bringing it between his golden lips to suck on it. Arslan's free hand wandered up to begin undoing the Windsor-knot tie, pulling it free and tossing it over his shoulder. He moved closer, teasing bites on Gabriel's palm as his free hand began to work on the buttons of the man's shirt. Thick, curly black hair covered Gabriel's dark chest when Arslan revealed it, and with the sound of a hungry animal Arslan pulled himself tight into the crowded embrace of Charlotte.

"Share," Arslan said in a playfully demanding tone, nibbling on Gabriel's ear. Charlotte smiled through her kisses and nudged Gabriel to turn his face to Arslan. If Charlotte's kiss had been a gentle breeze, Arslan's powerful and insistent kiss was like a tornado as he pushed himself into Gabriel, tongues playing with each other like Grecian wrestlers on a tropical holiday. Arslan's hand went down the front of Gabriel's trousers at the same time he squeezed the man's buttocks with the other. Charlotte took her lead from him and grabbed the other cheek. The alchemist was panting against them both, his need hard and strong.

Charlotte tugged at the ivory and gold corset of Shamhat, and the automaton released her, gently pricking each human with her lustful venom to enhance their experiences before skittering away to let the lovers love. With Shamhat gone, Charlotte pulled the cord of her black bustier in a way that released her. She pulled away slightly as Arslan and Gabrielle kissed, both to admire Gabriel's rock-hard cock pressing at his trousers begging to be free and to undo her scarlet flight leathers. She took Gabriel's free hand and brought it up to her soft breast as she shrugged the flight suit down to her waist. The alchemist moaned into his kiss with Arslan as the Doll slowly stroked his cock in the trousers. Charlotte kissed Gabriel's dark nipples, and threaded her hands through his thick chest hair, kneading it like a cat. Her mouth moved down his chest to his stomach.

The tip of Gabriel's erect penis, lighter than the shaft, was peeking out from the top of his pants while Arslan stroked it, and Charlotte playfully licked it. The pre-cum was hot and salty, and she could feel Gabriel about to orgasm. To forestall it, she quickly pressed a nerve point, allowing him to hold on a little longer. It had been a long time since Gabriel had been intimate with either a man or a woman, and it showed in his eagerness.

Arslan finally broke his hungry kiss and went to his knees, pulling Charlotte the rest of the way with him.

"Shall we give him what he wants?" Arslan teased with a knowing smile. Charlotte answered in kind, and together they pulled Gabriel's pants down.

Freed from its wool prison, the alchemist's cock stood rigidly out, a dark-brown shaft with an impressive thickness, the head protruding from his foreskin. Although it was only of average length, the girth made Charlotte's pussy wet with imagining it in her. It stood proudly and ready at face-level for both Arslan and Charlotte.

Arslan threw off his jacket and shirt, revealing his chiseled ivory body as Gabriel shrugged out of coat and shirt as well. Arslan's nipples were the same gold as Tash's, but where she'd had full curves, his chest was a thickly muscled hard body, barely softened by the magic animating him.

The Doll gripped the shaft of Gabriel's cock at its base, pressing one of his fingers on the nerve to intensify pleasure. Slowly, teasingly, he brought his lips to the head. Charlotte followed his lead, and they nearly kissed as they both suckled on the cockhead, each licking as they did so. Gabriel shuddered and moaned, ready to cum at any moment. But Charlotte knew they weren't done yet, and applied the pressure point again at his chakra.

After a solid minute of the head-sucking tease, Arslan took the entire length in with his mouth, giving Gabriel a hot and wet hole. Arslan moved his tongue as he sucked hard on Gabriel's cock like a starving man. Slowly, he moved his head back, and Charlotte began sucking and licking on the base of Gabriel's shaft again. Rather than go on to other techniques, the pair sucked and nibbled on Gabriel's cock in a regular, rhythmic pattern they shared.

When the orgasm came, neither of the tantric practitioners moved to stop it. Gabriel roared as he pushed

Arslan's head into the blowjob. Charlotte gave the boys their fun, but snaked a sudden finger into Gabriel's ass to stimulate him in the middle of it, weaving a spell of lubrication around the rim as a safeguard.

Arslan kept sucking as Gabriel filled his mouth with cum, semen dripping out from the edges as the alchemist came like he never had before in his life. He shuddered in orgasmic ecstasy, emptying his balls as he face-fucked Arslan in a savage, triumphant act.

But as he started to relax Charlotte tapped the base of his spine and sent a tendril of magic through. Rather than become flaccid, Gabriel's cock stayed erect, bypassing the too-sensitive stage right after orgasm as well.

"We're not done with you," Charlotte grinned, standing and unfastening her flight suit completely and stepping out of it to stand naked and proud before him. Her own skin was the middle ground between Gabriel's darkness and Arslan's paleness, a tawny brown that deepened at her nipples. Her bush was well tended with its curly locks, and she brought Gabriel's hand to it as Arslan also stood and pulled off his trousers.

Although the Doll had an impressive cock, longer and thicker than Gabriel's, the pale rod held little interest for Charlotte. She was more concerned with how Gabriel's fingers began moving in her pussy, the furtive, almost shy touches as he rubbed her clit with his thumb and slid his middle and ring fingers inside her, the wetness from her desire allowing easy entry. Charlotte pulled him close against her naked breasts as his fingers found the perfect spot inside her, the patch of skin that most men didn't even believe existed. She bit Gabriel's neck to keep from crying out as he used his two fingers to stroke her while his thumb massaged her clit.

Arslan used the distraction to slowly move behind Gabriel, nibbling and biting on his chest, shoulder, then back areas. He pressed his naked cock in between Gabriel's cheeks, the hardness a sultry question. Gabriel reached behind to Arslan's head and pulled him in, guiding the Doll into nibbling on his neck harder.

Charlotte stepped away, pulling Gabriel's fingers out of her pussy.

Without a word, she went to her knees in front of Gabriel. But instead of taking his cock in her mouth, she turned, going to her elbows and waggling her ass provocatively. Gabriel realized what they had in mind as Arslan applied gentle pressure to his upper back, encouraging him to bend over.

Gabriel, fully in the grips of lust, went to his knees on the temple floors, which were soft and gentle to the touch. He put his hands on Charlotte's hips, as Arslan went to his knees behind him and did the same. The alchemist hungrily pulled Charlotte toward him, penetrating her inviting warmth. Arslan licked his hand and stroked his pale cock before placing its tip against Gabriel's mystically-lubricated anus. There was a question, a permission asked in his hesitation.

The alchemist thrust back, forcing Arslan's cock into his ass. Arslan took the hint and slowly began thrusting into Gabriel, holding onto his hips with a firm but loving grip as Gabriel slid into Charlotte. They fell into a rhythm together, with Gabriel thrusting into Charlotte as Arslan pulled back, before drawing back as Arslan thrust forward into his ass. There were no words for a while, only the rhythm of thrusting, and the three felt time slow as they fucked each other's minds away.

Charlotte felt the satisfaction of the alchemist's thick cock penetrating her, and she grunted encouragement as she reached between her legs to her clit, stroking it in time to the thrusts. Gabriel, penetrating and being penetrated, thrust back and forth as he experienced the best of both worlds. Arslan's sexual venom was carried in his pre-cum deep in Gabriel's ass, enhancing the experience and making the alchemist hunger for more, for it all.

Their pace started to increase, and Charlotte could feel everyone building to a climax. She and Arslan were using small magic cues to time their sex, keeping the thrusts in perfect rhythm. Gabriel was too lost in lust and need to notice them subtly controlling the act, but he noticed when Charlotte put both of her hands behind her back, hiking her ass a little higher in the air. He took the proffered hands and restrained them, picking her up and suddenly starting to thrust as deep as he could into her. Arslan moved one hand up to the alchemist's shoulder, sending a jolt of magic through as the other hand held tight to Gabriel's ass.

"Yes," Charlotte moaned, both because she wanted to as well as encouraging Gabriel on. "Yes, fuck me, fuck me, FUCK ME!"

With each word she demanded more, deeper penetration.

"Do you feel me?" Arslan whispered roughly into

Gabriel's ear. "Feel my cock spreading your cheeks, feel me fucking you in the ass, filling you up?"

The pair's words made Gabriel thrust faster, wordlessly roaring as he gave himself completely over to fucking.

Three sets of screams echoed across the temple as they came at the same time.

"Yes, oh God, yes!" Gabriel managed to say through the ecstasy as he came in Charlotte's pussy at the same time Arslan came in his ass. Then he lost the capability of speech in the beautiful insanity of the threesome.

The sexual drug that the clockwork courtesan carried was transmitted with his semen, and suddenly Gabriel found himself cumming again, and again, lost to a world of desire as the jizz from the Doll caused him to orgasm again and again.

Gabriel fell to his side with heaving breaths, his cock pulling out of Charlotte's filled pussy with a slick sound as Arslan's dick fell limply from his ass. Gabriel was still rock-hard from Arslan's semen, but he was suddenly too sensitive, his skin a thousand warmths of the afterglow of sex, and this time Charlotte didn't smooth it away with magic. Even now, his cock was still coming, even though his balls had been completely emptied inside Charlotte.

There was an audible click behind them as the Engine of Eros was released by the temple in a way that seemed as if the complex itself had just climaxed as well.

Chapter 6

Charlotte didn't need her perceptor monocle to know how much sexual energy they had just released. On a sudden whim though, she reached between her legs, bringing the mixed taste of Gabriel and her pussy to her lips. She could feel the energy still coursing in the juices.

"You got this?" she asked Arslan, who had moved to support and hold the dry-coming Gabriel, whose eyes had rolled back in his head.

"I will tend to him until the venom wears off," Arslan said, nodding. "And, Captain? Thank you. You had every right to have him for yourself, and it would have still generated enough energy."

Charlotte laughed as she rubbed her sticky finger across the shattered engine pillar of Shamhat's and then, after a moment's consideration, across the Ereshkigal one. The Engine containing Ishtar's essence floated in place where it had been detached, waiting the attention of the Enkidu. "I wouldn't do that to you," she said, redirecting the fading energies into the ruined engine and then the pillar missing most of its data diamonds. With a little luck, she mused, they could screw up the Matriarchy's plans even more.

"Still. Thank you."

Charlotte smiled as she continued to weave the magic into the two Engines. She thought to herself that she should have guessed. Arslan had been asleep for thousands of years.

He'd had the worst case of blue balls in history.

Everyone was a little bit of an asshole when they were horny and frustrated. Charlotte finished directing the waning sexual energies into the Ereshkigal pillar before sitting back down and scooting over to where Arslan cradled Gabriel.

"Is he still out of it?" she asked, noticing that Gabriel had finally closed his eyes. Arslan held him close, gently stroking the alchemist's arms and legs as he readjusted the energy flows in Gabriel's body.

"Indeed," Arslan nodded, concentrating more on his work than the conversation. "My sexual venom is every bit as potent as Tash's, and I was not holding back. I'm actually quite impressed with his mental resiliency. He still has his mind. With how much…magic…I pumped into him, most would be little more than a slave dog to me now. According to the flows I'm seeing, he is still his own man."

Charlotte drew her legs into a sitting position after a short incantation that cleaned hers and Gabriel's mixed fluids off her with a small puff of smoke. The tantric aviatrixes had learned long ago how to tidy up quickly after the work. At a nod from Arslan, she did the same for the two men before settling back.

"Why do you and Tash have it though? The venom, I mean," Charlotte asked. "At first, I thought she'd been developed by the Legion of Lilith to enslave the world. But you're thousands of years old. So why does the Kurian-style frame have that feature?"

Arslan held Gabriel close, letting the darker man slumber on his ivory chest while tenderly stroking his close-shorn hair.

"To be honest, I'm not exactly sure," Arslan said, showing no signs of strain as he supported the other man gently. "I imagine it was to enthrall your people at first. After all, humans don't have a pleasant response to the unknown. I wasn't in the first colony wave, so I can only guess at the reasons why."

"Colony?" Charlotte asked, narrowing her eyes in suspicion. "You wanted to take the land for yourselves."

Arslan laughed, a pleasing baritone as rich as pipe smoke. "No, not like you think. We were curious. And the more curious we got, the more of us that wanted to make the transition."

"I don't understand. Do you mean you were a different sex before your current form?"

"No," Arslan said, shaking his head. "Nothing like that. In fact, we didn't know what sex was until we discovered you. Or rather, we had forgotten, our biological roots being an untold number of ages past."

Thinking of how Ereshkigal had posed as Godmother for decades, Charlotte said, "Were you without form in your original life, then? Do your people have to take empty shells as bodies?"

Arslan laughed again. "Oh no, we definitely had bodies. What do you think the Enkidu are based on?"

Charlotte's jaw dropped open in surprise. "Seriously?

Those giant manticore-looking things with too many fingers and an eyeless head? Those were your bodies?"

Arslan nodded. "After a fashion, yes. In truth, I don't think there's any of my people who remember our original forms. Immortality has a way of drifting your memories. But after we discovered you, the Enkidu frames were relegated to worker sprites. We created a body to resemble yours. I believe my people fell in love with humans and their potential. As I said, I wasn't in the original wave."

"And the addictive venom was how you chose to express that love?" Charlotte asked skeptically.

"I believe they were afraid of being rejected," Arslan said with an uncomfortable shrug. "After the Atlantis rift collapsed—"

"Wait! Are you saying the legend of Atlantis is real?"

Arslan looked annoyed she had interrupted. "Of course, it was real. The pioneer wave took control of the drowned bodies of sailors on the sea floor and constructed a complex to stabilize the rift. Only after the complex was done did we discover humans lived out of the ocean. We were…not wise in the ways of biological entities. After that it was a simple case of building proper bodies to interact with. The initial incursions out of the sea were disastrous with the Enkidu frames. We were mistaken for monsters, and tales of the 'manticore' arose. So, they redesigned our bodies into this."

"So, Atlantis was never actually on the surface?"

Arslan shook his head. "No, not at all. In our second expedition from the ocean floor, we came in the forms that your people came to call Kurian, dwellers of their mythical underworld, never realizing that the monsters they fled from the first time was an approximation of our first true bodies. Tales different Kurians told of Atlantis fueled the subsequent creation of the myth. As we shared basic technological improvements with our chosen host cities the legend spread that we were advanced humans, either from the underworld or the disappeared land, intermixed. Which, of course, was as far from the truth as you can get."

Charlotte nodded in understanding at his explanation. Although she was fascinated by his tale, she was splitting her focus between Arslan and the pillars. She could feel the seconds ticking away as Godmother and the Matriarchy forces closed in on them. She quickly got dressed before offering her hand to Shamhat, who took the proffered limb and crawled around to her back before once more forming into an ivory and gold corset. Giving an experimental shove to the floating Ishtar pillar, Charlotte found it still too heavy to move manually, barely budging an inch from her exertions. There was no way to move it without the Enkidu, so instead she turned her attention to Ereshkigal's pillar. The gold surface had turned to a liquid held in suspension with the infusion of magic. The pillar hadn't clicked free, but even if it had done so the captain had no room on her ship for two of the massive Engines. So, she did the next best thing to stymie Godmother's plans.

A whispered incantation and a touch to the pillar sent ripples through the golden medium holding the remaining data diamonds. The golden liquid was warm to the touch, yet did not stick to Charlotte's fingers as she manipulated the low-level magic she'd infused the Engine with.

The remaining data diamonds began to move over the surface, slowly all coming together to jumble up where the aviatrix's fingers worked the gold. Each diamond was about the size of her palm and plucking them out of the pillar's surface was as easy as picking an apple from a tree. A couple went into her pockets, but she soon realized there were too many gems to carry herself. Instead, she dragged Gabriel's backpack over, stuffing them into the already-full pack. All told, there were just thirteen data diamonds. But each one she pilfered was less strength in Godmother to chase them.

"Oh, yes," Arslan said dryly with lidded eyes. "This strikes me as a good idea."

"I'd rather Gabriel have them than Godmother," Charlotte said. "At least until we fly over the ocean again and I can send them to the bottom. Although, come to think of it, that might not be the smartest idea according to your tale. Fuck it. Volcano it is. Magma should make quick work of them. Even if they're not destroyed it should at least keep them out of reach, right?"

"I suppose that could work," Arslan nodded. "Extreme heat like that might even scramble the data-ents inside. Or maybe our man here has some sort of alchemical concoction that will dissolve them."

"Maybe," Charlotte allowed, fastening the pack again. "But he has other plans than destroying them. Still, better than Godmother. She's already inhabiting a floating city. The last thing we need is for her to regain her full faculties."

"On that we are in agreement," Arslan said.

There was the sound of clanking as Arslan called the Enkidu in from the hallway. The giant machine moved without hesitation to take hold of the released Engine containing Ishtar. Whereas Charlotte had barely been able to nudge it, the construct easily removed it from the mounting bracket. The Enkidu raised up on its hindlegs, moving the Engine around to its back. Three pairs of smooth pincers slid out of its ivory carapace, taking hold of the pillar and carrying it upon its back as a mother spider would with its eggs. It lowered itself back down, and stood there, awaiting directions.

"Did Jackson behave himself while we were indisposed?" Charlotte asked. Arslan cocked his head, silently querying the giant construct and receiving a reply.

"The sights of this temple are lost on him," Arslan replied with a disappointed sigh. "He is where we left him in the hallway, picking his nails with a knife. No trace of curiosity or wonder in his demeanor."

"At least Gabriel had a reprieve from the man for a little while," Charlotte said, nodding to the sleeping alchemist. "Do you mind carrying him? I'll gather his clothes and take his pack."

"Of course, it is no trouble," murmured Arslan, gently laying down Gabriel so the automaton could get dressed. Once he was clothed Arslan bent down once more, carefully lifting Gabriel as he stood up. The Black man's skin stood in contrast with the pale artificial man. After rummaging in his pack for a moment, Charlotte found a blanket to drape over the alchemist's nudity. Then she carefully put his glasses back on the slumbering man.

"Best not to give a free show to Jackson," Charlotte said, briefly touching old scars on the alchemist's upper arms and back. Although she had not noticed them during the lovemaking, in addition to the wooden arm both his feet were replaced as well. "Why does he keep that creature around? Jackson, I mean."

"You're a human; you would know better than I," Arslan shrugged.

"I suppose a further punishment," Charlotte guessed. "Or to keep him from hurting others. Maybe it's just for company, no matter how vile. Gabriel lost his crew, including any friends or loved ones, in the trip through the Bright. Despite his hateful nature Jackson represents Gabriel's last link to his past."

"No," Arslan disagreed. "His scars are wounds enough to remind him of those times. The other reasons I accept. But not the last."

Charlotte gave a short, bitter laugh. "You get to be the one to ask. I'm not touching the subject with a ten-foot pole."

The automaton and aviatrix followed the Enkidu out to the hallway, where they did indeed find Jackson just idling time. He began to bluster a little, but a sharp look from Arslan and the clank of the big Enkidu made him go pale and shut his mouth. Although Gabriel was still sleeping and thus incapable of hurting him via the botanical organs in his body, there was something to be said about good old-fashioned physical intimidation.

The azure-lit walls of the hallway felt less alien this walk through them to Charlotte. There was a pulsing warmth to the illumination she could feel now. Her mistake had been to assume the temple was some dead ruin, when it had a life of its own, even without Shamhat directly controlling it. What creatures were these Kurians that they could build such wonders without thought? What was their world like that they had forgotten the bonds of flesh until reminded?

"So…" Charlotte said with a rolling tone, savoring the word for all it was worth. "It's a bit of a walk to the ship. Care to talk about your world?"

"You are a direct creature, aren't you?" Arslan grinned. But then the grin faltered. "I suppose I can't just fob you off with a 'you would not understand' line, can I?"

"Nope," Charlotte grinned, excited that she had not been rebuffed out of hand.

"Very well," Arslan sighed. "But understand that when I say there are things you won't understand, it's not a mark against you. There are things beyond you right now."

"Stretch my mind," Charlotte demanded playfully.

For a few moments Arslan was silent, obviously organizing his thoughts.

"The first thing to understand," he began. "Is that we were once flesh."

"Yeah, the Enkidu forms, I remember," Charlotte said impatiently.

"How we came to be thought-forms is something that even the oldest of us struggle to remember. We existed in a shifting state of intermingled souls with our goddess watching over us. We created our own divine when the world failed us: Ereshkigal."

Charlotte nearly tripped over her feet in surprise. "You *created* her?"

"Well, not me, personally," Arslan laughed. "Did you not wonder what she was?"

"I just assumed she was a Kurian that got out of hand, or had delusions of grandeur," Charlotte said, struggling to comprehend the enormity of what he was saying.

"Not at all," Arslan continued. "She, like Ishtar and Shamhat, is an artificial creature, dreamt up by our greatest minds when we were still flesh. Or rather, she is the child of the children of the first artificials. They began to design themselves, and soon outstripped the confines of our intellect."

"Machines making machines," Charlotte said with wonder. "But, wait, you called her a goddess."

Arslan shrugged. "It is the closest approximation you would understand. A being of near-limitless effective power that expected to be worshipped as such. I'm not sure whether anyone remembers when we left the flesh behind, and whether it was our choice or not, but somehow during that time such a thing happened. We became immortal, living within the world Ereshkigal created for us. It was, by all witnessed, a paradise of infinite thought and simulated joy."

"But somehow you came to know this world?" Charlotte asked.

"It was Ereshkigal who found you," Arslan replied. "She grew bored of being the goddess of only one world. She began to research how to contact others, as the universe beyond our sphere was too remote to ever explore. It is difficult to put into your words the immense distance between worlds, and the difficulty such a thing entails, even for immortals. Bereft of the ability to expand out, Ereshkigal instead looked within. Other worlds had been theorized, dimensional planes below ours, but it took a bored goddess to punch through."

Charlotte was enraptured by the story. Jackson had tuned out entirely, walking beside them with a dull look on his face. Gabriel stirred in the automaton's arms but did not awaken. Charlotte resolved to memorize as much as she could about the tale, as Gabriel's unquenchable curiosity would demand to know all.

"You are aware of the four standard dimensions you exist in, yes?" Arslan asked.

"Four?" Charlotte asked with a cocked head. "Width, height, length, and…?"

"Time," Arslan finished.

"Oh, of course," the aviatrix said, feeling foolish. She should have guessed; after all, even sexuality existed along a timeline, fluidly moving as the person experienced more and tastes changed.

"Well, to put it bluntly: there are more."

"More dimensions?" Charlotte asked, cocking her head. "How many more?"

"It's not so simple as to be defined by a numerical value, at least not as you understand them. Suffice it to say, there are more, worlds upon worlds that interact with each other only with such an ethereal connection that to describe it in your terms can only be the divine."

The aviatrix felt like she should be insulted by the insinuation; but there was a matter-of-fact way that Arslan said it that seemed to be immutable fact rather than insulting. Even as he hinted at the fullness of further explanation, Charlotte could feel her mind struggling. She was no mathematician, but she vaguely recalled lessons from Godmother in her youth that had hinted at such things. Once more she found herself mystified why Ereshkigal would ever bother trying to educate or protect an orphaned child. Was she just one more distraction for a bored goddess, or had the intelligence harbored some sinister ulterior motive? It was impossible to answer.

"I think you may be right," Charlotte admitted as they left the lighted corridors of the temple proper and entered the shadowed launching cavern where the Matriarchy had once built pieces of Godmother's massive frame. "Right now, my mind is filled to the brim with what you've told me, and its implications on both the sisterhood and my own life. For now, I think I've got enough to grapple with. But we will return to this later."

Arslan bobbed his head. "As you wish. If you manage to understand even half of my story without ascribing it to gods, you would still be ahead of most others of this age."

"I rather enjoyed it," murmured Gabriel as his eyes fluttered open. "I would be receptive to hearing additional details."

Arslan's laugh was deep and heartfelt. "How much of that did you actually hear?"

"Enough to hunger for more," Gabriel said with a smile. "But as much as I enjoy you carrying me, I would like to get dressed."

Arslan kissed the alchemist on the forehead before

lowering him down. "Of course, Gabriel. Jackson, turn away, or I will pluck your eyes out before your next breath."

The former slaveowner snorted. "As if I'd like to watch him like your little f—"

Before he could utter the pejorative Arslan snapped into action, spinning him around and smashing his face into the rocky cavern wall.

"I do not like that word," Arslan said, golden lips curving with a grim smile. "If you enjoy possessing teeth, you will keep civil speech in that mouth of yours."

Jackson grunted and struggled to no avail, his head and body firmly pushed into the rocks.

"He never learns," Gabriel muttered with a head shake, taking the proffered clothes from Charlotte and dressing himself. "Don't bother with trying. No amount of words can teach a closed mind. Even pain only goes so far as the memory."

"Ah, but there is a deliciously wicked glee to turning the tables on his kind," Arslan said. "To hurt the one that hurts others has an intoxicating touch to it. Are you sure I cannot take a few teeth for good measure?"

"I never said you couldn't," Gabriel said. His tone softened and he laid a hand on Arslan's back. "But you would be less if you did. And that I do not wish."

Arslan nodded, letting Jackson out of his dangerous clutches.

"Let's see how long the dog behaves," Arslan said, a dark and violent look withering the bluster that Jackson tried to summon. "It would be in your best interest to stay silent around me, filth. I have had more than my fill of you and your kind through time immemorial."

The strange procession exited the temple proper with its immaculate walls and glass floors into the launch cavern. Dim light glowed from the engraved runes and manticores on the walls, casting the entire cave in a bluish hue. But that was a vast improvement from before, when a mystic leeching field had drained both the *Harlot's Promise* and all of Charlotte's machines of energy.

Charlotte whispered an incantation and sent a pulse of weak magic through the cavern. For a moment, nothing happened, and the captain began to despair. But then one, another, and then another tiny orb reacted to her call. The fae lights she'd used to illuminate the space and that had died on her in the leeching field each rose, their colors swishing in a dazzling display as they arced back to their mistress. Charlotte gave a delighted little cry that they weren't dead, feeding more magic into them, creating a weaving tapestry of glowing lights as the tiny constructs orbited her like a hive of fireflies around their queen.

"Beautiful," Gabriel whispered, reaching out to one of the fae lights. Charlotte slowed it down and directed it to land on the alchemist's outstretched hand. He let out a small laugh, his eyes wide with wonderment.

"I think Arslan's venom is still having an effect on you," Charlotte laughed. "These were some of my first creations. I still have a few from my days as a teenager."

Gabriel shook his head to clear it, but the smile remained.

"I suspect you are right, Captain," he admitted. "But I

wager they're still as wonderous even if I wasn't drunk off of our romp."

Charlotte shared his smile before sending the fae lights spinning off in the direction of the *Harlot's Promise*. The illumination from the tiny flying marbles lit the airship, casting soft shadows from where it sat on its landing struts. The Liberty Ship was a work of art, from bow to stern having an elegant curve edged in faux gold over the crimson hull. The control ruby on Charlotte's brow glowed as she established connection with her ship. Twin pontoon engines on either side twisted one way then another like a woman stretching her legs. The propellers spun rapidly before cycling down, ready to obey their mistress's commands.

When Charlotte had left the *Harlot's Promise* the airship had been in a sorry state, having lost her seaward sail with cracks running across her battered frame. But the Enkidu had been hard at work, and the missing sail had been replaced with another, folded up across the ship's belly like a tail curled around a sleeping fox. Charlotte could feel the unhealed wounds in the libidium frame through the control gem, hurts that would take time in drydock to mend. But she didn't have the months needed to repair. As distressed as the *Harlot's Promise* was, it remained their only hope of escape from the incoming Matriarchy ships.

"Hmm," Charlotte mused, stroking her chin. "I think we have a problem here."

The Enkidu waited patiently behind the captain as she mentally calculated the sheer volume of the Engine of Eros it carried. The diamond-studded column was massive, even if it was affected by the weight-negating magic that ran through the Kurian machines.

"Do you not have a hold to store the Engine in?" Gabriel asked.

"I do, but the problem is getting it into the cargo hold without ripping my ship apart," Charlotte answered. "We could strap it down on the foredeck, but it would be naked and defenseless against any attacks we suffered. Then again, I'm not sure how long the ship will even hold out. Shamhat warned me that the longer we fly, the greater the chance that the *Harlot's Promise* will simply shake herself apart."

"Every minute we take to think about it brings the Matriarchy that much closer," Arslan pointed out.

"Well, fuck it," Charlotte said with a heavy sigh. "We'll crash before too long anyway. Strap that thing to the foredeck and hope. With a little luck we can make it a few hundred miles before we shake the ship apart."

At Arslan's silent command the giant Enkidu strode up to the *Harlot's Promise*. Reaching onto its back the trio of prongs holding it in place slid away as it lifted the Engine containing Ishtar off. The Enkidu gently placed the pillar on the deck of the airship before skittering back into the shadows.

"All right, everybody up the ramp," Charlotte ordered, shooing them forward. "We've still got to secure the Engine. Arslan, can you be a dear and unseal the cavern so we can get the hell out of here?"

Arslan gave her a mock salute, but the easy grin with it reassured Charlotte that he was simply being playful. Gabriel hurried aboard with her, matching step with step as they hurried aboard. Jackson looked dubiously at the grounded ship, scratching his unshaven chin, before shrugging and slouching up the boarding ramp.

Charlotte led the way up the winding interior stairs, bypassing the hold and living areas before coming out on the deck.

"There's some rope in that chest over there," she directed, nodding at a firmly anchored box to the left of the starward mast.

"On it," Gabriel said, flipping the latches up on the chest and muscling the coiled rope out.

Wordlessly Charlotte started helping him uncoil it, throwing the rope over the Engine of Eros before tightening the rope around the belaying loops on the deck. They crisscrossed it with as much rope as they could, but she still had her misgivings on whether the diamond-studded pillar would stay put. She wasn't exactly sure how the Kurian magic worked, and even though the libidium that allowed the *Harlot's Promise* to fly was based on the same technology she wasn't sure how it would interact with the flying field.

There was a crack sound like thunder above, and then the grinding of millennia-old mechanisms as the roof of the cavern split into two. Bright noonday sunlight pierced the darkness of the cavern as the twin slabs rumbled apart. Dirt and plant matter showered down, but not so much as the first time the roof had been opened. Charlotte finished fastening down the Engine as the sunlight from the opening roof shone down fully onto the *Harlot's Promise*.

"Come on, baby," the captain whispered to her ship,

sending tendrils of her consciousness into the damaged craft. "We need to fly."

There was an unholy groaning noise Charlotte had never heard from the Liberty Ship before, and she didn't leap off her landing struts. But, slowly, haltingly, the ship rose a foot off the ground. The landing struts retracted, and Charlotte braced for any crash. But there was none, and despite the wobble in her floating, the captain could feel the *Harlot's Promise* ready to soar.

"All right, Shamhat," Charlotte said, rubbing her fingers on the mechanical corset. "Time for you to do your magic."

Clarification: you wish to activate Enkidu reserves?

"Yes. Release the hounds."

There was a tremor at the boundary of sensation as Shamhat communed with the Temple of Ishtar. The *Harlot's Promise* began ascending, steadying out as Charlotte fed more power into the libidium frame. Below, the freed Enkidu leapt for the ship, but came up short. The sounds of glass floors shattering as the army of Enkidu mobilized was deafening. Shamhat had been true to her word: to land now in the Temple of Ishtar was to face death head-on.

The sound of someone hacking a phlegmy spit distracted the aviatrix from her task. Jackson had come up on deck and was spitting on the ship itself with a leering grin at her. He knew exactly what he was doing, and the disrespect for the Liberty Ship and its captain was writ bold across his weathered features.

"I tire of you, Jackson," Gabriel said, pushing his glasses up in a contemplative gesture. "I had hoped a life divested of your prior crimes would demonstrate a real person underneath. This I did because I was asked by a man I respected. But I disagree with his base premise: evil is something that seeps into your bones, and no amount of clean living can erase it, especially if that decent life is forced upon you."

Charlotte was only partially keeping track of the conversation, so it took her split attention a moment to notice that Gabriel had brought his fist up. Jackson doubled over in sudden agony, not even able to utter a scream.

"For years I spared your life, the last connection to my past," Gabriel whispered. "But that time is over. The automaton was right: you violate any place you stand, tainting it with your grimy soul. And I think it's about time to solve that."

Gabriel unclenched his fist, holding it palm down. Jackson went rigidly upright. Gabriel mimicked walking with two fingers. Jackson lurched to the side, hitting the railing of the deck. Charlotte tried to yell out, but before she'd drawn breath Gabriel had jerked his hand up.

Jackson threw himself over the railing of the ascending airship into the mass of rampaging Enkidu as they poured out into the cavern in a mindless rage.

The old slaveowner found time for just one terrified scream.

And then he was silent.

Chapter 7

"What the hell is wrong with you?" Charlotte yelled, still splitting her attention between the ship and Gabriel.

"You were right," he said with a shrug. "I shouldn't have kept him. Part of me wanted to torture him to death over the years. But a clean cut is best to keep the wound from being infected."

"I said you should get rid of him, not that you should kill him!" Charlotte said. "We could have ditched him at the nearest town or something. But you fed him to the Enkidu!"

Gabriel's tone was apologetic, but his cruel action had thrown Charlotte for a loop. Gabriel didn't look like a man who'd just committed murder, but it didn't change the fact he'd used his magic to kill someone. It made Charlotte sick to her stomach.

"Just…just go down below decks," she muttered, trying to reconcile the alchemist with his actions. "I can't…we're about to be in battle. I can't look at you right now."

Gabriel shrugged, darkness clouding his features. "Should I regale you with the horrible stories of what Jackson did? Would that help you to digest this more easily?"

"Lilith's tit!" Charlotte cursed. "Have you heard nothing I've said? You used magic, the lifeblood of the world, to kill someone."

"Technically, I just made him jump," Gabriel said, spreading his hands. "The Enkidu are what killed him."

"No!" Charlotte spat. "It's the same thing. You might as well have stopped his heart. He's dead because you used magic on him. Just...go below deck. I can't afford the distraction."

Gabriel stuck his jaw out stubbornly, but a sharp look from Charlotte cut off any more protestations. His gaze lingered on the Engine of Eros strapped to the bow, his fingers twitching unconsciously, longing to explore the power locked within. But he wasn't willing to risk Charlotte's temper. He retreated down the stairway, leaving the captain alone on the deck.

The *Harlot's Promise* cleared the twin slabs of the cavern roof, bursting out into the blazing heat of the Syrian desert. The cavern rumbled closed behind the ship, for all the good it would do. There was little chance that Godmother couldn't just command it open again. But at least her prize was being spirited away.

As she brought the ship to a hover, Charlotte reached out again with her mind and started the pontoon engines. The propellers spun rapidly, and the *Harlot's Promise* moved slowly ahead, gaining speed every moment. For a moment Charlotte just let herself enjoy the feel of the air on her skin and the hull of the ship. An aviatrix regularly split her senses between her Liberty Ship and herself, and the experience of diving through the air with the twinning was exquisite.

But all too soon reality interrupted the dream. Through the ship's sensors she saw a trio of vessels arcing toward the *Harlot's Promise*. She dialed in the magnification and saw two blue-hulled enemy airships and one that was a deep shade of purple with green stripes running through it. The two blue ships she didn't know; their hulls had elegant lettering marking them as the *Concubine* and the *Azure Angel*. But she didn't need to see the purple ship's name. It was all too familiar to her: *Lilith's Revenge*. It belonged to the woman that had played a crucial part in breaking Charlotte's marriage and heart.

Major Erin Enright.

The airship was a mirror of her captain, a blocky thing lacking elegance and grace, well-suited to brutality instead of beauty. It wasn't designed like the Liberty Ships, instead taking war as its prime imperative. The deck was shrouded in a cowl of protective wooden planks, angled to deflect bullets and other projectiles, with additional armor placed across the sides. Liberty Ships traditionally relied on stealth and speed to avoid conflict as much as possible. Abusers would return home to simply find their victims absent. But Major Enright had advocated for a more direct approach and modified her ship for it. Yet as satisfying as it would be to knock teeth out of mouths, Charlotte, like most Liberty Ship pilots, understood that the mission was to save lives. It would endanger the very lives they were dedicated to saving to wade into the morass openly and violently. Enright would consider it as acceptable losses. It was one of the many thoughts of hers that Charlotte found abhorrent. That her ex-wife, Lauren, chose to betray her trust and continue the tryst with the Major stung even now, months and leagues later.

There was a burst of static from the speaker located on the mast of Charlotte's ship, nearly making her jump out of her skin. It was easy to forget the radio vox unit, as the only one who usually spoke to her through them was Godmother. There was a sudden pang of longing, of missing the artificial woman. Godmother had been the closest thing to family that Charlotte had, no matter what Sumerian goddess she actually was.

"Char, can you hear me?" Major Enright's voice crackled. "Char, come in."

Charlotte suppressed a shudder. "Char" had been Lauren's pet name for her. Enright kept trying to use it, and every time it made Charlotte grit her teeth. It was like nails on a chalkboard now thanks to her. If she never heard the name again, it would be too soon.

There was a sudden air pressure change, and a dark violet beam blazed across the starboard bow. Charlotte had been expecting stun beams like the enforcers were equipped with. But whatever had just been shot at the ship was altogether different. The energy pattern she could see through the airship's sensors registered something more than four times the strength of the stunner beams. She's always suspected that the Legion was working on armaments, but the beam confirmed it.

They had weaponized pleasure to a deadly degree.

One hit by the main cannon on the *Lilith's Revenge* was strong enough that were it to hit an organism, it would likely overload their nervous system. It would have been kinder to use a firearm or cannon. Dying from overstimulation would be a hellish fate for anyone.

Another beam was fired past the ship, this one close enough to glance off the invisible flying field. There was a wobble in the flight before Charlotte managed to stabilize the flows again.

"You are ordered to stand down," Erin's voice crackled over the speaker. "Look, I don't really give a fuck whether you do or not. But Godmother wants us to take you alive. Her little favorite. But if you don't respond you'll leave me no choice but to shoot you out of the air."

Once more Charlotte was drawn back to the central question: why? Why had Ereshkigal raised her, kept her safe, taken a personal interest in an orphaned girl. There was no sense to it.

"I'm here," she finally replied to the vox unit under the speaker on her mast. "I'd say it's nice to hear from you, but I really hate lying. I see you've managed to pervert magic into a weapon. Good job."

"Yeah, the neural overpulse beam is a hell of a thing," Erin snorted at Charlotte's sarcasm. "I've been looking for a reason to deploy it. Thanks for that."

"Sure, anything for a friend," Charlotte shot back, sarcasm dripping on every word. "I'm surprised you got enough aviatrixes to go along with it."

"I can be very persuasive," Erin said smugly.

Charlotte was deliberately stalling for time while her mind raced. The trick she pulled on the enforcer flitters and their stun beams wouldn't work against this new weapon. The overpulse weapon would slice right through her flight field, even supercharged with sexual energy. The Legion's new weapon was too powerful to take head on.

Charlotte fully sank her senses into the *Harlot's Promise*, extending the starward and seaward sails to maximum and feeding all the power she dared into the pontoon engines. She cut transmission for a moment to the exterior vox unit to hide her plan.

"Hang on, down there," she said, projecting her voice through the speakers below decks. "This is going to be rough."

"Time's up," the speaker crackled with the Major's voice. "Surrender or die screaming. Seems like an easy offer to me."

Charlotte cut the speaker out entirely in response and slipped her feet into a pair of leather straps fastened to the deck. She reached out her senses; it was easy to feel the neural overpulse cannon charging. It was bleeding its energy signature, and Charlotte already had a measure of the intensity it fired. The split second before the beam fire she made her move.

The *Harlot's Promise* dove down like a hawk seeking its prey, the sudden movement catching Major Enright by surprise. The deadly overpulse beam sizzled through where the ship had been. Charlotte pulled out of the sudden dive, her legs feeling like they were going to collapse under the strain. Even though the flight field negated some effects of gravity and momentum, Liberty Ships weren't designed for such rough handling. All through the arc up Charlotte kept her attention on the overpulse weapon. There was no instant zap frying her ship. She could feel it slowly building power back up, and it made her grin. There was a cooldown on the weapon, and in that window she had a chance.

"You missed," she taunted the vox unit.

The laugh that answered caught her off-guard.

"Cute ballet moves," the Major complimented her. "How long can you keep it up? I've got fresh batteries and all the time in the world. What about you?"

"I can dance the night away," Charlotte lied.

In truth, new cracks were opening in the ship's libidium frame from the rough handling. From Charlotte's estimation of what she was feeling, the ship had one, maybe two more severe maneuvers left. Then she'd break apart like a rotten log, scattering its passengers out like so much dirt. Even now the captain could feel hull sections trying to wiggle their way from the superstructure.

The weapon was fully charged again, and Charlotte breathlessly waited for the energy signature. As soon as she felt the tell-tale release she put the *Harlot's Promise* into a hard ninety-degree turn, leaving the beam scorching the air where she had been.

A couple of the hull planks ripped free, pulled off the ship like a giant peeling an orange. Charlotte struggled to level out of the turn. Through her sense-link to the ship it felt as if her bones were all fractured to the point of breaking.

The next shot would be the end of the *Harlot's Promise*, one way or the other.

"I can't let them get the Engine of Eros," she whispered to herself, looking at the diamond-studded giant pillar where it rested on the foredeck. Charlotte spared a glance down to where Arslan and Gabriel huddled in the crew quarters. She envisioned the Kurian beauty that had stolen her heart, and a tear rolled down because she couldn't say farewell. "I'm sorry, Tash. I wasn't smart enough to come up with another plan."

Charlotte put the ship into a wide arc, trying to nurse the airship through her hurts as she turned to face her attackers. The *Concubine* and the *Azure Angel* immediately split off from the *Lilith's Revenge*, obviously fearing the very suicide run that Charlotte was plotting.

Major Enright laughed through the crackling speaker, but Charlotte ignored her and pushed as much speed as she dared through the *Harlot's Promise*. Bereft of any choice, there was still one option available to the aviatrix.

She was going to go out on her own terms.

With luck, the Engine of Eros containing Ishtar would be destroyed, as well as the data diamonds for the rest of Ereshkigal's mind. Charlotte suspected the items were too tough to be destroyed by something as pedestrian as a crash though. Still, if she managed to scatter the pieces over a wide enough area, at least then the world might have a chance to breathe before Godmother marshalled her lackeys.

"Nice try, Char," the speaker crackled. "But all you've done is give me a good target. It really is a shame. If you'd just listened to reason…ah, well. Spilled milk and crying and all that sort of nonsense."

Charlotte felt the energy buildup through the ship's sensors. She was still too far away. Pushing the *Harlot's*

Promise faster and faster took every ounce of energy she had. But it still wasn't enough.

They were about to get blown out of the sky.

With the adrenaline of certain death pumping in her veins time seemed to slow down. Charlotte saw the beam blast forth from the overpulse cannon mounted on the bow of the *Lilith's Revenge*. It ripped the air, leaving the atmosphere smoldering in its path. The beam struck faster than thought and Charlotte braced herself. She managed one last course correction, dipping the nose of the Liberty Ship again. It wasn't enough to dodge the bolt of ecstatic death, but it did mean the bolt would impact the Engine of Eros first, giving her the best possibility of destruction.

The energy beam struck the Engine and a flash of light brighter than the sun turned the world white.

A cracking boom and a wave of heat washed over Charlotte. She screamed in defiance, struggling to remain upright to meet death on her feet. But then something she'd never anticipated happened.

She lived.

The heat washing over her felt like it was going to cook her alive, and her sight was blanked out. But her blood did not boil, her flesh did not burn.

Ishtar's Engine of Eros had taken the energy blast full-on and somehow absorbed it.

Belatedly Charlotte tried to use the *Harlot's Promise* sensors to course-correct, but it was too late. Rather than smash into the *Lilith's Revenge* the force of the blast and the blinding of the blast had caused Charlotte to drift off-course. By the time she could make sense of the world through the ship's systems they were passing underneath the *Lilith's Revenge*, the top of the starward mast scraping a line in the belly-paint of the other ship.

Cursing, Charlotte gave the commands to bank back around. The *Harlot's Promise* was barely holding together, and there was zero chance that Erin wouldn't turn her ship around and blast the defenseless enemy craft again. But there was a sudden problem.

The *Harlot's Promise* wasn't responding to her commands.

Charlotte rubbed her eyes, trying to get back her sight. Her connection to the ship was going in and out in a way she couldn't explain. The captain could feel well enough that the foredeck had nearly been obliterated by the blast, but any information past a general unease was being blocked by something.

As her vision started to clear Charlotte gave a gasp. To her tortured sight it looked like the Ishtar Engine had been critically wounded. Instead of a solid pillar, the gold liquid had broken free of whatever field was containing it, draining into the blast wound around it, data diamonds moving like leaves on a raging river.

The aviatrix didn't know what to do. Her connection with the *Harlot's Promise* was fluttering like a stone skipping on the water, destined to drop into the water at any time. Charlotte fought the connection, trying to order the ship to come about for another try at ramming the *Lilith's Revenge*.

There was no change in their heading.

A strange feeling was being fed back into her mind from the ruby control gem on her forehead. A sensation of warmth was spreading through her limbs, a comfortable anesthesia of her hurts. No, not her wounds.

The ship's.

Charlotte realized with crystal clarity that the destroyed Engine of Eros was flowing into the cracks in the libidium frame, moving like a living thing as it infiltrated every nook and cranny of the nearly-broken airship. It had spread faster than she would have believed, not just to the blast wound on the foredeck, but into and through the skeleton of the ship. Even as she fought to regain mastery of the *Harlot's Promise* the ship slipped more and more out of her control.

Awakening protocols initiated: Ishtar.

The sudden words through her skin from Shamhat's corset took Charlotte by surprise.

"The goddess? Or the sprite or whatever you call it stored in the data diamonds?"

Charlotte assumptions: correct. Warning: awakening protocols damaged. Chances of successful initialization: zero point zero three percent.

"Seems like she's waking up just fine," Charlotte growled. "Bitch is taking over my ship."

Shamhat did not respond, and Charlotte got the impression the artificial intelligence had been offended by her words. But the aviatrix didn't care. They had their backsides to the *Lilith's Revenge*. They were about to die, with no chance to even the score.

The all too familiar feeling through the ship's sensors of the overpulse cannon charging made Charlotte despair. With none of the problems that faced the *Harlot's Promise* the enemy ship had already banked around and was running them down like a wolf on a stag.

Crackling surged through the speaker, and Charlotte readied for another gloating tirade from Major Enright.

"Brace," a hoarse and otherworldly voice said over static.

A sudden surge of speed nearly threw Charlotte out of the leather feet straps. The sizzling buzz of an overpulse beam shot through where they should have been, but by the time the beam had arrived the *Harlot's Promise* had darted to the right and down, doubling her speed. In the distance Charlotte saw the heavy outline of the Amythest City, glinting in the noon sun like a second purple star. The enforcer flitters that the trio of enemy airships had outrun were buzzing like angry hornets as they closed in.

"No!" Charlotte cried, trying to send commands through her control ruby to no avail. "Turn! Turn!"

The speaker crackled again with static.

"Turn."

The phantom voice did as it said it would, and Charlotte found herself nearly blacking out as the *Harlot's Promise* banked hard without slowing down. The aviatrix fought to stay conscious as the force drove her to her knees. Just as she had directed it before, the ship lunged toward the enemy. But instead of heading right for the purple and green-hulled enemy the *Harlot's Promise* streaked underneath once more.

Another bolt streaked past, and Charlotte could almost swear she heard the gunner cursing as they tried to track the airship. The aviatrix turned her head to see the *Lilith's*

Revenge receding quickly behind them as the *Harlot's Promise* sprinted away. By the time the other ship could change its heading it would be too late at the speed Charlotte's craft was travelling. The captain tried connecting with the ship again through her control ruby, but there was a momentous pressure resisting her.

"Shamhat," she said above the keening wind that was penetrating the flight shield. "What the fuck has happened to my ship?"

Engine housing: damaged. Emergency infiltration: resultant. Your vessel: new Engine of Eros.

"The fuck it is," Charlotte growled. She stomped her boot on the deck. "Ishtar, is it? Would you mind kindly fucking back off to your pillar?"

There was no response from the speaker. The ship continued to barrel ahead at twice what should have been its top speed, showing no signs of slowing.

"Captain Frost?" Arslan called up from belowdecks.

Charlotte took a breath to control her rising anger. "Yes?"

"You'd better come down here," Gabriel said.

Chapter 8

The aviatrix tried to keep her temper under control, but she couldn't help but be irritated. She thought that there'd be some sign of the Ishtar infiltration in the beams.

But it was so much more than that.

Charlotte saw gold-filled cracks running through the luxurious mahogany of her stairwell like granite as she descended. In the crew quarters there were several places where there was more of the gold cracking than wood itself. Arslan and Gabriel were examining several of the cracks with interest.

"Something happened up top, didn't it?" Gabriel said, eagerness pressing in his voice. "What did you do?"

"What did *I* do?" Charlotte asked sarcastically. "I think we're well past what I tried to do, and deep in the territory of me being rather fucking annoyed at losing control of my ship."

Arslan had the ghost of a smile pass his lips.

"What happened?" he asked, weight to his words. "This gold looks rather familiar. Tell me you didn't."

"Didn't what?" Charlotte groused. "Try to make the best of a bad situation? Try to go down in a blaze of glory instead of being shot like a pheasant for dinner? Yeah, I tried those things."

"And in the process breached the Engine on the foredeck?" Arslan asked. There was a coolness to his words, a hidden serpent slithering behind.

"Oh, if it were only that simple," laughed Charlotte bitterly. "I managed to alter our course enough that the killing shot from that overpulse weapon hit the Engine. I thought it would blow, taking us all with it."

"How noble of you," Arslan said, his eyes lidded.

"I didn't see any way out. We were lined up for a kill shot," Charlotte said.

"And you're unhappy that Ishtar flowed out and saved us all?" Gabriel asked in a puzzled tone.

Charlotte took a deep breath, letting it out slowly as she struggled to bring her temper under control. "Yes…and no. Am I glad we're all still alive? Overjoyed. Leaping over the moon happy. Do I enjoy having no say or control of my own ship? Fucking guess, sugar."

Arslan ran his smooth white fingers over the golden filling in an overhead beam. "You really must speak to someone about your overwhelming urge to control every situation. It seems to me that this has turned out all for the best, after all."

"Yeah?" Charlotte asked, trying not to sneer. "I could say the same thing about Tash invading your body."

"What?" Arslan said, his tone carrying a dangerous weight.

"You heard what I said," the aviatrix retorted. "How's it feel having that extra passenger with you all the time? Are you tired yet of having an unwanted roommate? Feels bad to lose control, doesn't it? This is my ship. Mine! It's the only godforsaken good thing to remain of my marriage and life. And now this entity, this *thing*, has taken her from me!"

Arslan shot her a chilly glance. "And here we were getting along so well. I think I'd like to hear what Tash has to say to you about your viewpoint."

As his features started to shift to feminine, Charlotte harrumphed at him.

"That's it, go on, run. Easier than taking the truth head-on."

Even as Tash's delicate features softened Arslan's disappearing face her lips were pursed in a frown.

"Just when I thought the two of you were past such hostility," she said, her voice not even fully changed before she leveled the recrimination.

Charlotte threw her hands up. She was trying to control her temper, but everywhere she looked the gold-filled cracks seemed to have spread. She knew from her brief connection to the ship that the libidium frame was shot through with the material too.

"Where's the data diamonds?" Gabriel asked. "Did they shatter, or are we just missing them?"

"The…ah, hell," Charlotte said, realizing he was right. "Power core!"

Tromping down the stairs from the quarterdeck, Charlotte led the rest of her unusual group down to the battery banks, cursing at what she found.

Data diamonds were sealed against the battery banks like fruit on the tree. But as Charlotte tried to pry a diamond off there was no budge, no movement of any kind from the jewels. The entire power room, the heart of the *Harlot's Promise*, was covered in the data diamonds that contained Ishtar's essence.

"It looks like Ishtar has found a new home," Gabriel said, wonderment filling his voice. He was fascinated by the transition, and was examining and tugging on several diamonds, finding them snugly seated.

"This is not what I want," Charlotte protested weakly. The whole situation had spiraled quickly out of control, and she was flummoxed about what to do.

Gabriel took his glasses off, pulling out a cloth to clean them. He brushed off imaginary dirt before putting the spectacles back on.

"Want is such a weak word," he said. "What is, and what is necessary, are so much more than want. Needs. Needs are much stronger. Like the need to survive. I'm more familiar with that word and hold it in greater esteem. I did not want to do the things for my freedom that I did. But I needed to. You tried to suicide into the other ship, taking our choices away from us. How much did you consider what *we* wanted."

"I'll not stand here and be lectured by a murderer," Charlotte said with a savage tone.

"As you say," Gabriel said, inclining his head. "Feel free to go above and rage at the sky if it makes you feel better. But what I did to that man was as much need as want. You. You were the one who made me realize all I was doing was torturing both myself and him. He was a twisted recollection, a scar tissue I could not forget. You made me realize I could never truly move on until he was dead."

"I did not tell you to kill him," Charlotte growled.

"But you did, in your own way," Gabriel shrugged. "What did you think, that I was just going to let him go along on his merry way, unpunished? He was never leaving my service alive. Truth be told, I still believe he got off easy all things considered. I've got some truly hideous powders that would have made his final days unending agony. But you made me realize I was lessening myself by indulging those darker desires. In much the same way your churlish anger right now lessens you. You're striking out at anyone who doesn't immediately leap to your defense. You want people to pick sides. Well, I'm on the side that doesn't have us destroyed in a huge ball of fire. I'm on the side that keeps an ancient Sumerian deity out of the hands of zealots. That seems like a pretty good side to me."

Charlotte was so irritated all she could do was yell into her arm for a moment. Regaining her composure, she straightened her flight leathers and Shamhat corset.

"What do you think I should do?" she asked, all too sweetly. "Thank the golden goo that has seeped through my ship, taken it over? Is that your solution? Perhaps we should sacrifice some cattle to it, or the firstborn?"

Gabriel shrugged, leaning on his cane. "Why not talk to it, to *her*? You're trying to take back control by force. Have you even thanked Ishtar for saving our asses out there? I know you didn't truly want to die. Can you admit it to yourself?"

"I...you're right," Charlotte said, taking a deep calming

breath. "I did not want to die. I didn't see a way out. I'm just…honestly, I'm just a little frightened. We're deep into uncharted territory, even by Kurian standards. Did Arslan even know that the Engine could be breached like that?"

Tash cocked her head, as if listening to a sound no one else could hear. Then she shook her head.

"He did not. Apparently, humans haven't ever constituted a true threat, outside of being fooled into working with Ereshkigal."

"I thought as much," Charlotte nodded. "So, you'll excuse me if I get a little tetchy when an ancient Sumerian god merges with my ship. That sort of thing really puts you out of sorts."

"Is she truly awake though?" Gabriel asked. "Could the transition have damaged her?"

"That…is an excellent question," Charlotte allowed. "Give me a moment."

Closing her eyes, Charlotte measured her breathing out with pranayama, purging the lingering hostility in her emotions. Then calmly, gently, she reached out once more through the control ruby to the ship. The overwhelming pressure of Ishtar's presence was there, blanketing the connection like wet cloth over a mouth.

"Ishtar?" she murmured. "Are you there?"

There was the impression of a huge thing moving in her mind through the connection, like feeling the ground shake as an elephant passed by. The speaker in the crew quarters started emitting heavy static, and above it came one word.

"Yes."

"Are you undamaged?" Charlotte asked.

There was a pause.

"No."

The captain shared a worried look with the other two.

Charlotte swallowed her pride to ask the real question.

"Can you please relinquish control of the *Harlot's Promise* back to me?"

Again, there was the impression of a massive beast moving, a glacier passing in the night. The pressure resisting her lessened but did not disappear. Still, Charlotte was able to access the flight controls, pulling back on the speed the ship was going, from twice her normal to a more reasonable cruising speed. Several parts felt damaged by the over-acceleration. A little more time and there would have been permanent wounding of key systems.

"Unable. More," crackled the speaker.

Charlotte nodded in understanding. The infiltration of her ship had been an emergency reaction, trying to find a new suitable vehicle for the mighty intelligence that resided in the Engine of Eros. Now that her temper had cooled off somewhat, she understood that the transition had not been one of intentional malice. What must have the destruction of her container seemed like to Ishtar? How much was she aware of when confined to the Engine? When considered in that light, infecting the *Harlot's Promise* was an act of preservation, not hostility. And Charlotte was enough woman to admit the Kurian intelligence had saved the ship when the only way out seemed to be death.

Now that Charlotte could properly perceive the ship's status through the psychic connection, she could feel how much stronger the beams and structure were. Where before she was frightened of taking a turn too rapidly, now she could sense that the former upper limits of speed and maneuverability were able to be exceeded. By how much, she couldn't say, but the *Harlot's Promise* was stronger than before by an unknown magnitude. Although it was nearly all internal changes, the fact of the matter was that the Liberty Ship was likely the fastest thing in the entire world now.

Always at the edge of her perception there was that massive presence lurking. But Charlotte could also sense that Ishtar was holding back, doing her best to allow the aviatrix to take control of the ship. There was a new balance, a new normal to adjust to. For both of them. What must the world seem like to an entity that had slumbered for a millennium?

"It's all right," Charlotte whispered, projecting her words through the connection. "Rest. Regain yourself. We'll talk later."

There was the impression of relief filling her mind before it withdrew back into itself. Charlotte could feel that she had control of the ship again, even though Ishtar's influence lurked like a boulder teetering above. The Kurian intelligence had done its best to relinquish as much of her new body as she could. The *Harlot's Promise* was no longer completely under Charlotte's command, and she knew she'd have to get used to this new paradigm. But based on the speed and maneuverability she'd witnessed there were upshots to having a Sumerian goddess co-piloting the ship.

"Better, Captain?" Gabriel asked.

"Just about," Charlotte said. "We should give her some time to rest. Let's go up on deck."

Gabriel cocked his head questioningly, but both he and Tash followed the aviatrix back up the stairs.

The wind was blunted by the flight field, but there was still enough slipping through to tousle their hair as the ship flew forward. Down below, the Ottoman Empire sprawled like some great creature, and their passage likely elicited more than one disruption to the day's activities. The sun was over its apex, and in a few hours daylight would disappear, giving way to the darkness once more.

"Where do you want to go, Gabriel?" Charlotte asked, turning to the alchemist.

The man was taken aback by the question. "I, uh, don't really know. I've been looking for the Engines for the last several years. It never occurred to me that such unique circumstances would surround them. I thought of them merely as power sources, something I could take and return to my people with. Something I could use to free them. I hesitate to ask you to ford the Bright with me. It is a dangerous and uncertain trip."

Charlotte shook her head with a sad frown. "You misunderstand me, Gabriel. I asked you where you want to be dropped off. You will not be accompanying us anywhere else."

"Is this about Jackson?" Gabriel asked, worry lining his features.

"Of course it is," Charlotte responded, her tone firm. "You used magic to murder a man. I cannot overlook that, no matter how pleasant your company might be."

"But—" Gabriel started to say.

"No," Charlotte said louder, cutting him off. "This is not a negotiation. I will not entertain you in this. No matter the explanation, the fact remains you perverted the lifeblood of the world to kill. There's no getting around that."

"And what would you have had me do?" Gabriel asked, visibly frustrated.

"I don't know," Charlotte admitted. "Hell, I might have even been able to forgive you just pushing him out of the ship as we flew away. There's no way to know. But you used magic. You soiled it. Speaking of…Tash? Can you do me a favor and go down to check his pack and remove the data diamonds I stashed there?"

The automaton nodded, leaving the pair as Gabriel kept struggling to change the captain's mind.

"Have I committed such a crime on a man who did things a hundred times worse to me and my people?" Gabriel said bitterly.

"I can't judge you," Charlotte admitted. "I am not without sin myself, nor am I some priest or preacher. But I do know the things I cannot forgive. For that, you must face the consequences. No matter what you say or do, you crossed a line. A big one."

"Are you so intent on being alone for the rest of your life?" Gabriel asked, sourness tinging his voice. "You push everyone away, logic and reason away anyone who would be close to you. How long until Tash or Arslan perform some unforgivable deed to you? Will you even tell them, or just abandon them and fly away, sure in your rightness and isolation?"

Charlotte shook her head. "I'm sorry you feel that way. I really am. And there is some truth to your words. I need to be more open about what I feel and what hurts me, lay out the map for people to avoid stepping in a hidden bear trap. But none of that applies to you. I'd made my feelings about perverting magic quite clear when you were just torturing Jackson. Do you think that murder is somehow better? Did you think I would just accept it?"

Gabriel shook his head. "You're just bound and determined to be alone, aren't you?"

Charotte took a deep breath, then blew it out, steadying her nerves.

"You can't talk me out of this," she said, not unkindly. "This is not easy on me. But I would not be the woman I am if I let such an egregious act go unrebuked. I cannot predict the future. I don't know that I won't end up alone and miserable, as you say. But I know my values, and I know how I feel right now. I cannot simply overlook this or forgive you. Magic should not be used to kill. That is a treasured foundational principle of mine. And no matter how attractive you might be, no matter your reasoning, no matter how justified it might be, that was a bridge too far. I'm sorry you don't understand it, but that doesn't change what must be."

"Oh, I understand it, all right," Gabriel said tightly, his teeth gritted. "You will be alone and miserable, Charlotte Frost. In the end, your principles will be the only thing you have left against the cold night."

"Maybe," Charlotte allowed with an uneasy shrug. "Maybe not. But I cannot betray who I am for anyone. Not you. Not Arslan. Not even Tash. In the end, we are all alone with our choices, even if someone warms our bed. If you cannot live with yourself, then there's no way you'll be happy with someone else."

Gabriel gave a grunt of frustration, turning and leaning on the railing of the deck. Charlotte understood his displeasure. She had lost her relationship with Lauren after her wife had crossed a line, same as him. And there was an aching loneliness under the surface, a need to be close to someone. But if she did not hold up her own ideals, then who would she be? Could she look in the mirror without hating a part of herself if she let things like lies and murder slide? Would she have her soul at the end of the day if the things she held most sacred were tossed away so easily?

Charlotte stared off in the distance, her mind set, even as her heart ached at her choices.

Staying true to herself was perhaps the greatest cost and the greatest reward at the same time. But any other choice would make her a woman she did not know, could not live with.

The horizon rushed forward, as did both the threat and the promise of the future.

About the Author

Award-winning author Timothy Black was born in the Deep South where he hit the road at an early age and quickly learned it could hit back. Driven by an insatiable curiosity, he studied Geology, Astronomy, and the Occult, ending up with a degree in Philosophy that twists through his writing. After traveling the world to find his great loves he settled down in the Pacific Northwest, determined to craft stories that defy confinement to any single genre. A serial killer of coffee and whiskey sours, he stays one step ahead of retribution with a rebellious cackle and knowing wink.

Facebook: facebook.com/timothyblack.author/
Twitter: @Tim_RFP

The Tales of the Tantric Aviatrix
The Clockwork Courtesan
The Ishtar Ignition
The Engines of Eros

Gearteeth
Published by Dreamsphere Books
Gearteeth
Judgment of Blood

Also by Timothy Black
Published by Dreamsphere Books

Gearteeth
Timothy Black

On the brink of humanity's extinction, Nikola Tesla and a mysterious order of scientists known as the Tellurians revealed a bold plan to save a world ravaged by a disease that turned sane men into ravenous werewolves: the uninfected would abandon the Earth's surface by rising up in floating salvation cities, iron and steel metropolises that carried tens of thousands of refugees above the savage apocalypse.

Twenty years later, only one salvation city remains aloft, while the beasts still rule the world below. Time has taken its toll on the miraculous machinery of the city, and soon the last of the survivors will plummet to their doom. But when Elijah Kelly, a brakeman aboard the largest of the city's Thunder Trains, is infected by the werewolf virus, he discovers a secret world of lies and horrific experiments that hide the disturbing truth about the Tellurians.

When the beast in his blood surges forth, Elijah must choose between the lives of those he loves, and the city that is humanity's last hope of survival.

Available in ebook and paperback!